J.E.

"Well. That was…unexpected."

Sage's color was high but she didn't look upset by their heated embrace, only surprised.

Eben, on the other hand, was stunned to his core.

What the hell was he thinking? This kind of thing was not at all like him. He was known in all circles—social, business or otherwise—for his cool head and detached calm. He had spent his life working hard to keep himself in check.

The urgent heat for an exotic, wild-haired nature girl sent him way, *way* out of his comfort zone.

"My apologies," he said, his voice stiff. "I'm not quite sure what happened there."

"Aren't you?" Sage asked.

Dear Reader,

For our first home together, my husband and I bought a Queen Anne Victorian built in 1904. We loved the grace and character of it—the high ceilings, the intricate moldings, the gingerbread trim. We weren't quite as crazy about the single-pane glass windows (painted shut!), the crumbling mortar and the lack of closet space.

We spent fifteen years in that house—refinishing wood floors, scraping off layer after layer of paint and wallpaper, replacing those wavy-glass windows with versions that had less charm but a great deal more energy efficiency.

As much as we loved our old house and poured our hearts into it, eventually we had to build one that met our family's needs a little better.

When I was creating Brambleberry House, I took all my favorite things from our little redbrick Victorian—and all the elements I might have wished it had!—and incorporated them into the walls of the old house.

I hope you enjoy exploring the secrets of this sprawling mansion by the sea and the women who call it home.

All my best,

RaeAnne

THE DADDY MAKEOVER

RAEANNE THAYNE

SPECIAL EDITION®

Published by Silhouette Books

America's Publisher of Contemporary Romance

SILHOUETTE BOOKS

ISBN-13: 978-0-373-24857-5
ISBN-10:   0-373-24857-1

THE DADDY MAKEOVER

Books by RaeAnne Thayne

Silhouette Special Edition

Light the Stars #1748
Dancing in the Moonlight #1755
Dalton's Undoing #1764
**The Daddy Makeover* #1857

Silhouette Romantic Suspense

The Wrangler and the Runaway Mom #960
Saving Grace #995
Renegade Father #1062
**The Valentine Two-Step* #1133
**Taming Jesse James* #1139
**Cassidy Harte and the Comeback Kid* #1144
The Quiet Storm #1218
Freefall #1239
Nowhere To Hide #1264
†*Nothing To Lose* #1321
†*Never Too Late* #1364
The Interpreter #1380
High-Risk Affair #1448
Shelter from the Storm #1467
High-Stakes Honeymoon #1475

*Outlaw Hartes
†The Searchers
**The Women of Brambleberry House

RAEANNE THAYNE

finds inspiration in the beautiful northern Utah mountains, where she lives with her husband and three children. Her books have won numerous honors, including a RITA® Award nomination from Romance Writers of America and a Career Achievement award from *Romantic Times BOOKreviews* magazine. RaeAnne loves to hear from readers and can be reached through her Web site at www.raeannethayne.com or at P.O. Box 6682, North Logan, UT 84341.

Chapter One

On a scale of one to ten, Sage Benedetto would probably rate the concept of jogging before sunrise every day somewhere around a negative twenty.

While she highly doubted she would ever evolve enough that she could wholly enjoy these runs, after a month, she had at least grown to tolerate the activity. Her gut didn't automatically cramp at just the idea of throwing on her running shoes and her muscles no longer started to spasm after the first few steps.

She supposed that was a good thing.

This would probably never be her favorite thing to do, but she *had* promised, she reminded herself. And while she had many faults—all of which somehow seemed more glaringly obvious in the pale light of early morning—breaking her word was not among them.

Despite the random muscle aches and her inherent dislike of just about any activity that involved sending her heart rate into heavy exertion mode, she had even come to discover an ethereal beauty in these quiet early-morning runs.

The towering sea stacks offshore glowed pink in the first, hesitant rays of the sun; this wide, gorgeous stretch of Oregon beach was empty, at least for a little while longer.

Soon the beach would be crowded with treasure hunters looking for shells or colored glass or any other gift the sea surrendered during the night. But for now it was hers.

Hers and Conan's, anyway.

A huge red beast emerged from behind a cluster of rocks and shuffled to her, scaring up a seagull.

She sighed. This was the reason she was here before sunrise, her thigh muscles burning and her breath sawing raggedly. This rangy, melancholy creature was her responsibility, her curse, her unexpected legacy.

"There you are. You can't keep slipping off your leash or we won't do this anymore."

Abigail's big mutt, rescued from the pound right around the time Abigail rescued Sage, cocked his head and gazed at Sage out of doleful eyes the murky dark green of the sea in a November storm.

Some days these jogs along the shore seemed to lift his

spirits—the only reason she carried on with them when she would much rather be home in bed for another hour.

This apparently wouldn't be one of those days.

"I know," she murmured, rubbing his chin as she slipped the leash back on. "She loved these kind of mornings, didn't she? With the air clear and cool and sweet and the day just waiting to explode with possibilities. Anything-can-happen days, that's what she called them."

Conan whined a little and lowered himself to the sand, his head sagging to his forepaws as if he were entirely too exhausted to move.

"You've got to snap out of it, bud. We both do."

She tried to swallow down the lump of grief that had taken up permanent residence in her throat during the past month. Her eyes burned and she wondered when these raw moments of sorrow would stop taking her by surprise.

She blinked away the tears. "Come on, dude. I'll race you home."

He gave her a long, considering look, then heaved to his feet and shuffled off in the direction of Brambleberry House, still a mile down the beach. Even at his most ponderous pace, Conan could outrun her. A pretty sad state of affairs, she decided, and tried to pick up her speed.

Focusing on the sand in front of her, she had only made it a few hundred yards down the beach, when she heard a sharp bark. She turned in the direction of the sound; Conan was at the end of his long retractable leash, sitting with a small figure above the high-tide mark in the sand.

The figure was a young girl, one she wasn't even sure was old enough to be considered a tween. A young girl who was wearing only a pale green nightgown and what looked to be seashell-pink flip-flops on her feet.

To Sage's deep surprise, Conan's tail wagged and he nudged at the girl's hand in a blatant invitation to pet him. She hadn't seen Conan greet *anyone* with this kind of friendly enthusiasm for the better part of a month.

Sage scanned the beach looking in vain for the girl's companion. She checked her watch and saw it was barely 6:00 a.m. What on earth was a young girl doing out here alone on an empty stretch of beach at such an hour, and in nightclothes at that?

"Morning," she called out.

The girl waved. "Is this your dog?" she called to Sage with a big smile. "She's so pretty!"

Conan would just love being called pretty. When he wasn't grieving and morose, the beast had more prickly pride than a hedgehog with an attitude. "*She's* a *he*. And, yeah, I guess you could say he's mine."

Partly hers, anyway. Technically, she shared custody of the dog and ownership of Brambleberry House. But she wasn't about to let thoughts of Anna Galvez ruin one of Abigail's anything-can-happen days.

"His name is Conan," she said instead. "I'm Sage."

"Hi Conan and Sage. My name's Chloe Elizabeth Spencer."

The girl had short, wavy dark hair, intense green

eyes and delicate elfin features. If she'd been in a more whimsical mood, Sage might have thought her a water sprite delivered by the sea.

A cold, wet breeze blew off the Pacific and the girl shivered suddenly, drawing Sage's attention back to her thin nightgown and her nearly bare feet. "Chloe, what are you doing out here by yourself so early?"

She shrugged her narrow shoulders with a winsome smile. "Looking for sand dollars. I found four yesterday but they were all broken so I thought if I came out early enough, the tide might leave some good ones and I could get them before anybody else. I promised my friend Henry I'd bring one back to him and I can't break a promise. He lives in the apartment next door. He's only seven and won't be eight until December. I've been eight for two whole months."

"Where's your mom or dad? Do they know you left?"

"My mom's dead." She said the words in a matter-of-fact way that Sage was only too familiar with. "She died when I was six."

"What about your dad, then?"

"I'm not sure. He's probably still asleep. He got mad at me last night because I wanted to find more sand dollars so I decided to come by myself this morning."

Sage looked around at the few isolated cottages and guesthouses on this stretch of beach. "Are you staying close by? I thought I knew all the eight-year-olds in town."

"Every one?" With a lift of her dark eyebrow, the

girl somehow managed to look skeptical and intrigued at the same time.

"I do," Sage assured her. "The ones who live here year-round, anyway. I'm sure I don't remember meeting you."

Cannon Beach's population was only a couple thousand year-round. In the summer, those numbers swelled as tourists flocked to the Oregon shore, but they were still a week or so away from the big crowds.

"We're only here for a few days. Maybe a week. But if it's longer, then my dad says he'll have to send me to stay with Mrs. Strictland so he can get some work done. She's my dad's assistant and she hates me. I don't like going to her house."

Though she knew it was unfair to make snap judgments about a man she had not even met, a clear image of the girl's father formed in Sage's mind—a man too busy to hunt for sand dollars with his motherless child and eager to foist her on his minions so he could return to conquering the world.

She fought down her instinctive urge to take Chloe home with her and watch over her like a sandpiper guarding her nest.

"Do you remember where you're staying, sweetheart?"

Chloe pointed vaguely north. "I think it's that way." She frowned and squinted in the opposite direction. "Or maybe that way. I'm not sure."

"Are you in a hotel or a condo?"

The girl shook her head. "It's a house, right on the

beach. My dad would have liked to stay at The Sea Urchin but Mr. Wu said they were all booked. He didn't look very happy when he said it. I think he doesn't like my dad very much."

No wonder she had always considered Stanley Wu an excellent judge of character. She hadn't even met Chloe's father and already she disliked him.

"But what I don't get," the girl went on, "is if he doesn't like my dad, why is he going to sell him his hotel?"

Sage blinked at that unexpected bit of information. She hadn't heard Stanley and Jade Wu were considering selling The Sea Urchin. They had been fixtures in Cannon Beach for decades, their elegant boutique hotel of twenty or so guest rooms consistently named among the best accommodations along the coast.

"Do you know if your rental is close to The Sea Urchin?"

Chloe screwed up her features. "Pretty close, but I think it's on the other side. I didn't walk past it this morning, I don't think."

Though she seemed remarkably unconcerned about standing on wet sand in only her nightgown and flip-flops, she shivered a little and pulled Conan closer.

Sage sighed, bidding a regretful goodbye to any hopes she might have entertained of enjoying a quiet moment for breakfast before heading to work. She couldn't leave this girl alone here, not when she apparently didn't have the first clue how to find her way home.

She shrugged out of her hooded sweatshirt and

tucked it around Chloe's small shoulders, immediately shivering herself as the cool ocean breeze danced over her perspiration-dampened skin.

"Come on. I'll help you find where you're staying. Your dad will be worried."

Conan barked—whether in agreement with the plan or skepticism about the level of concern of Chloe's father, she wasn't sure. Whatever the reason, the dog led the way up the beach toward downtown with more enthusiasm than he'd shown for the ocean-side run. Chloe and Sage followed with the girl chatting the entire way.

In no time, Sage knew all about Chloe's best friend, Henry, her favorite TV show and her distant, work-obsessed father. She had also helped Chloe find a half-dozen pristine sand dollars the gulls hadn't picked at yet, as well as a couple of pieces of driftwood and a gorgeous piece of translucent orange agate.

"How do you know so much about shells and birds and stuff?" Chloe asked after Sage pointed out a surf scoter and a grebe.

She smiled at Chloe's obvious awe. "It's my job to know it. I'm a naturalist. Do you know what that is?"

"Somebody who studies nature?"

"Excellent! That's exactly what I do. I work for an organization that teaches people more about the world around them. When I'm not working on research, I get to show people the plants and animals that live here on the Oregon Coast. I even teach classes to kids. In fact, our first nature camp of the summer starts today. That's how I know so many of the local children, because most of them have been my campers at some time or another."

"Really? That's so cool!"

She smiled back, charmed by the funny little creature. "Yeah, I think so, too."

"Can I come to your camp?" The girl didn't wait for an answer. "My dad has another hotel in Carmel. That's in California, too, like San Francisco where we live. Once I went with him there and my nanny took me to see the tide pools. We saw starfish and anemones and everything. It was *super*cool."

Her nanny, again. Did the girl's father even acknowledge she existed?

"Did you at least tell your nanny where you were going this morning?" she asked.

Chloe stopped to pick up a chipped shell to add to the burgeoning collection in her nightgown pockets. "Don't have one. Señora Marcos quit two days ago. That's why my dad had to bring me here, too, to Cannon Beach, because he didn't know what else to do with me and it was too late for him to cancel his trip. But Señora Marcos wasn't the nanny that who took me to see the tide pools anyway. That was Jamie. She quit, too. And the one after that was Ms. Ludwig. She had bad breath and eyes like a mean pig. You know what? I was *glad* when she said she couldn't stand another minute of me. I didn't like her, either."

She said this with such nonchalance the words nearly

broke Sage's heart. It sounded like a very lonely exis-
tence—a self-involved father and a string of humorless
nannies unwilling to exert any effort to reach one energetic little girl.

The story had a bitterly familiar ring to it, one that
left her with sick anger balled up in her stomach.

None of her business, she reminded herself. She was
a stranger and didn't know the dynamics between
Chloe and her father. Her own experience was apropos
of nothing.

"Does any of this look familiar?" she asked. "Do
you think your beach house is close by?"

The girl frowned. "I'm not sure. It's a brown house
made out of wood. I remember that."

Sage sighed. *Brown* and *made of wood* might be
helpful information if it didn't describe most of the
houses in Cannon Beach. The town had strict zoning
laws dictating the style and aesthetics of all construc-
tion, ensuring the beachside charm remained.

They walked a little farther, past weathered cedar
houses and shops. Sage was beginning to wonder if
perhaps she ought to call in Bill Rich, the local police
chief, when Chloe suddenly squealed with excitement,
which prompted Conan to answer with a bark.

"There it is! Right there." Chloe pointed to a house
with an unobstructed view of the ocean and the sea
stacks. Sage had always loved the place, with its quaint
widow's walk and steep gables.

"Are you sure?" she asked.

Chloe nodded. "I remember the fish windchimes. I heard them when I was going to sleep and it sounded like angels singing. And I remember the house next door had those big balls that look like ginormous Christmas ornaments."

Sage shifted her gaze to take in the collection of Japanese glass fishing floats that adorned Blair and Kristine Saunders' landscape.

"Do you have a key?" she asked the girl.

Chloe held tight to Conan's collar. "No. My dad didn't give me one. But I climbed out the window of my room. I can just go back that way."

Sage was tempted to let her. A quick glance at her watch told her it was now twenty minutes to seven and she had exactly forty minutes to change and make it in to work. Her life would certainly be easier if she let Chloe sneak into her rental house, but it wouldn't be right, she knew. She needed to make sure the girl's father knew what Chloe had been up to.

"We'd better make sure your dad knows you're safe."

"I bet he didn't even know I was gone," Chloe muttered. "He's going to be mad when he finds out."

"You can't just sneak out on your own, Chloe. It's not safe. Anything could have happened to you out on the beach by yourself. I have to tell your dad. I'm sorry."

She rang the doorbell, then felt like the worst sort of weasel when Chloe glared at her.

Before she could defend her action, the door opened and she forgot everything she intended to say—as well as her own name and how to put two words together.

Chloe neglected to mention the little fact that her father was gorgeous. Sage swallowed hard. The odd trembling in her thighs had nothing to do with her earlier run.

He had rugged, commanding features, with high cheekbones, a square, firm jaw and green eyes a shade darker than his daughter's. It was obvious he'd just stepped out of the shower. His hair was wet, his chest bare and he wore only a pair of gray trousers and an unbuttoned blue dress shirt.

Sage swallowed again. Why did she have to meet a man like him *today* when she smelled like wet dog and four miles of sweat? And she already disliked him, she reminded herself.

"Can I help you?" he asked. She didn't mistake the shadow of irritation on those rugged features.

She blinked and tugged Chloe forward.

"Chloe?" he stared at his daughter, baffled concern replacing annoyance. "What's going on? I thought you were still sound asleep in your bed. What are you doing out here in your nightgown?"

She didn't answer for a moment then she shrugged. "Nothing. I just went for a walk to get some more sand dollars. I found a ton. Well, Sage helped me. Look." She thrust her armload at her father.

He didn't take them, gazing at his daughter's hard-won treasure with little visible reaction. Or so Sage thought, until she happened to catch the storm clouds scudding across his green eyes like a winter squall stirring up seafoam.

"What do you mean, you went for a walk? It's barely six-thirty in the morning!"

Chloe shrugged. "I woke up early but you were still sleeping and I didn't want to wake you up. I was just going to be gone for a minute, but…then I couldn't remember how to get back."

"You are in serious trouble, young lady."

His voice was suddenly as hard as a sea stack and Sage was automatically seven years old again, trying desperately to understand how her world could change with such sudden cruelty.

"I am?" Chloe's fingers seemed to tighten on Conan's collar but the dog didn't so much as whimper.

"You know you're not supposed to leave the house alone. You *know* that. *Any* house, whether our own or a temporary one."

"But Daddy—

"You promised me, Chloe. Do you remember that? I knew bringing you along on this trip would be a huge mistake but you promised you would behave yourself, for once. Do you call running off down the beach by yourself behaving?"

He didn't raise his voice one single decibel but muscles inside Sage's stomach clenched and she hated it, hated it. The terrible thing was, she couldn't blame the man. Not really. She could imagine any parent would be upset to discover a child had wandered away in an unknown setting.

She knew it was a normal reaction, but still this particular situation had an entirely too-familiar ring to it.

"But I wasn't alone for very long," Chloe insisted. "I made two new friends, Daddy. This is Sage and her dog's name is Conan. She lives here and she knows all kinds of things about birds and shells and fish. She's a naturist."

"Naturalist," Sage corrected.

"Right. A naturalist. She teaches summer camp and tells kids about shells and birds and stuff like that."

For the first time since she rang the doorbell, the man shifted his gaze to her.

"I'm Sage Benedetto," she said, hoping her cool voice masked the nerves still jumping in her stomach. Though she wanted to yell and scream and ask him what the hell he thought he was doing trying to quash this sweet little girl's spirit, the words tangled in her throat.

"I live down the coast about a half mile in the big Victorian," she said instead.

He stared at her for a long second, an odd, arrested look in his eyes. She didn't know how long he might have stared at her if Conan hadn't barked. The man blinked a little then closed his fingers around hers.

She was quite certain she imagined the odd little sizzle when their fingers touched. She *didn't* imagine the slightly disconcerted expression that crossed his features.

"Eben Spencer. Thank you for taking the time to bring my daughter home."

"You're welcome," she said in that same cool voice. "You might want to keep a closer eye on her."

"Easier said than done, Ms. Benedetto. But thank you for the advice."

"No problem."

She forced a tight smile for him, then a more genuine one for his daughter. "Bye, Chloe. You need to rinse those sand dollars in fresh water until the water runs clear, then soak them in bleach and water for five or ten minutes. That way they'll be hard enough for you to take them home without breaking. Remember, Henry's counting on you."

The girl giggled as Sage called to Conan, who barked at her, nuzzled Chloe, then bounded off ahead as they headed back toward Brambleberry House.

He watched her jog down the beach, the strange woman with the wild mane of honey-colored hair and thinly veiled disdain in her haunting amber-flecked brown eyes.

She didn't like him. That much was obvious. He hadn't missed the coldness in her expression nor the way she clipped off the ends of her words when she spoke to him.

He wasn't sure why that bothered him so much. Plenty of people disliked him. Constantly striving to win approval from others simply for the sake of their approval wasn't in his nature and he had long ago learned some measure of unpopularity was one of the prices one paid for success.

He was damn good at what he did, had taken his family's faltering hotel business and through careful management, a shrewd business plan and attention to detail turned it into a formidable force in the luxury hotel business.

Over the years, he had bumped up against plenty of affronted egos and prickly psyches. But seeing the disdain in Sage Benedetto's unsettling eyes annoyed him. And the very fact that he was bothered by it only irked him more.

What did he care what some wind-tousled stranger with a massive, ungainly mutt for a dog thought of him?

She stopped at a huge, cheerful yellow Victorian with incongruent lavender trim some distance down the beach. He watched her go inside and couldn't stop thinking about that odd jolt when their hands had touched.

It was completely crazy but he could swear some kind of strange, shimmery connection had arced between them and he had almost felt as if something inside him recognized her.

Foolish. Completely unlike him. He wasn't the sort to let his imagination run wild—nor was he the kind of man to be attracted to a woman who so clearly did not share his interest.

"She's nice. I like her. And I *love* her dog. Conan is so cute," Chloe chirped from inside the room and Eben realized with considerable dismay that he still stood at the window looking after her in the early-morning light

He jerked his attention away from thoughts of Sage Benedetto and focused on his daughter. Chloe had spread her treasures on the coffee table in their temporary living room, leaving who knew what kind of sand and grime on the polished mahogany.

He sighed, shut the door and advanced on her. "All right, young lady. Let's hear it."

He did his best to be firm, his tone the same one he would use with a recalcitrant employee.

These were the kind of moments that reminded him all too painfully that he didn't have the first idea how to correctly discipline a child. God knows, he had no childhood experience to draw from. He and his sister had virtually raised each other, caught in a hellish no-man's-land between two people who had had no business reproducing.

Between their mother's tantrums and violent moods and their father's shameless self-indulgence, it was a wonder either he or his sister could function as adults.

Cami had found happiness. As for him, he was doing the best he could not to repeat the mistakes of his parents.

"You know the rules about leaving the house by yourself. What do you have to say for yourself?"

Chloe shifted her gaze to the sand dollars in front of her and he hated himself when he saw the animation fade from her eyes. "I'm sorry, Daddy. I promise I won't do it again."

Eben sighed. "You say that every time, but then you find some other way to cause trouble."

"I don't mean to." Her voice was small, sad, and he found himself wishing fiercely that he were better at this.

"I try to be good but it's so *hard*."

He had to agree with her. Nothing was as hard as trying to do the right thing all the time. Even right now, some wild part of him wanted to call up Stanley and Jade Wu and tell them to go to hell, that he didn't want their stupid hotel if they were going to make him work this hard for it.

That same wild corner of his psyche wanted to toss Chloe onto his shoulders and run out into the surf with her in his bare feet, to feel the sand squishing between his toes and the cold water sluicing over his skin and her squeals of laughter ringing in his ears.

He tamped it down, containing it deep inside. "Try a little harder, okay?" he said sternly. "This deal is important to me, Chloe. I've told you that. You've got to be on your best behavior. I can't afford any distractions. It's only for a few more days, then I promise when we get back to San Francisco, we'll find a new nanny."

She nodded, her little mouth set in a tight line that told him clearly she was just as annoyed with him as Sage Benedetto had been.

"I'm supposed to have meetings with Mr. and Mrs. Wu most of the day so I've made arrangements for a caregiver through an agency here. All I'm asking is for you to behave. Can you try for a few hours?"

She looked up at him through her lashes. "When you're done with your meeting, can we buy a kite and fly it on the beach? Sage said Cannon Beach is the perfect place to fly kites because it's always windy and because there's lots of room so you don't run into people."

"If you promise to be on your best behavior, we can talk about it after my meetings."

She ran to him and threw her arms around his waist. "I'll be so good, Daddy, I promise, I promise, I *promise*."

He returned her embrace, his heart a heavy weight in his chest. He hated thinking of her going to boarding school at the end of the summer. But in the two years since Brooke died, Chloe had run through six nannies with her headstrong behavior. Some sort of record, he was certain. He couldn't do this by himself and he was running out of options.

"Maybe Sage and Conan can help us fly the kite," Chloe exclaimed. "Can they, Daddy?"

The very last thing he wanted to do was spend more time with Sage Benedetto of the judgmental eyes and the luscious mouth.

"We'll have to see," he said. He could only hope a day of trying to be on her best behavior would exhaust Chloe sufficiently that she would forget all about their temporary neighbor and her gargantuan canine.

Chapter Two

"Sorry, Conan. You've got to stay here."

Sage muscled her bike around Anna's minivan and wheeled it out of the small garage, trying to ignore the soulful eyes gazing back at her through the flowers on the other side of the low wrought-iron fence circling the house. "You'll be all right. I'll come back at lunchtime to throw a ball with you for awhile, okay?"

Conan didn't look convinced. He added a morose whine, his head cocked to one side and his chin tucked into his chest. She blew out a frustrated breath. They had been through this routine just about every day for the past month and the dog didn't seem to be adjusting.

She couldn't really blame the poor thing for not

wanting to be alone. He was used to having Abigail's company all day.

The two of them had been inseparable from the moment Abigail had brought him home from the pound. Conan would ride along with Abigail to the shops, his head hanging out the backseat window of her big Buick, tongue lolling. He would patiently wait for her on the porch of her friends' houses when she would make her regular round of visits, would sniff through the yard while Abigail tended her flowers, would curl up every evening beside her favorite chair in front of the huge bay windows overlooking the ocean.

Conan was lonely and Sage could certainly empathize with that. "I'm sorry, bud," she said again. "I'll be back before you know it."

The dog suddenly barked, his ears perking up like twin mountain peaks. He barreled to the front porch just as the door opened. From her place on the other side of the fence, Sage watched Anna Galvez—trim and proper in a navy blazer and gray slacks—set down her briefcase to greet the dog with a smile and a scratch under his chin.

Anna murmured something to the dog but Sage was too far away to hear. She wasn't too far to see Anna's warm smile for Conan trickle away when she straightened and saw Sage on the other side of the wrought-iron.

She brushed hair off her slacks and picked up her briefcase, then walked to the gate.

"Good morning. I thought I heard you come down the stairs some time ago. I figured you had already left."

Sage straddled her bike, not at all in the mood for conversation. Her fault for sticking around when she heard the door open. If she'd left then, she could have been halfway to town by now. But that would have been rude and she couldn't seem to shake the feeling Abigail wanted her to at least pretend politeness with Anna.

"I couldn't walk out in the middle of his guiltfest."

"He's good at that, isn't he?" Anna frowned at the dog. "I expected him to be past this phase by now. It's been a month. Don't you think he should already be accustomed to the changes in his life?"

Sage shrugged. "I guess some of us need a little more time than others to grieve."

Anna's mouth tightened and Sage immediately regretted the low comment. So much for politeness. She wanted to apologize but couldn't seem to form the words.

"I wish I could take him with me to work," Anna said after an awkward moment.

Sage gave the other woman a disbelieving look. Anna couldn't possibly want a big, gangly dog wreaking havoc with the tchotchkes and whatnot in her book and gift shop in town. Conan would bankrupt her in less than an hour.

"I've been coming home for lunch to keep him company for awhile. Throw a ball, give him a treat. That kind of thing. For now, that's the best I can do."

For an instant, guilt flickered in Anna's brown eyes but she blinked it away. "I'm sorry. I should have realized you were doing so much. I'm a little preoccupied with some things at the store right now but it's only right that I do my share. Abigail left him to both of us, which means he's my responsibility as well. I'm sorry," she said again.

"Don't worry about it."

"I'm afraid I can't come back to the house today," she said with a frown. "But I'll try to arrange my schedule so I can take a few hours to be here with him tomorrow."

"I'm sure he would enjoy that," Sage said. As always, she regretted the awkwardness between her and Anna. She knew Abigail had wanted them to be friends but Sage doubted it was possible. They were simply too different.

Anna was brisk and efficient, her world centered on By-The-Wind, the shop she had purchased from Abigail two years earlier after having managed it for a year before that. Sage didn't believe Anna had even the tiniest morsel of a sense of humor—or if she did, it was buried so deeply beneath spreadsheets and deposit slips that Sage had never seen sign of it.

After two weeks of sharing the same house, though in different apartments, Anna was still a stranger to Sage. Tightly wound and tense, Anna never seemed to relax.

Sage figured they were as different as it was possible for two women to be, one quirky and independent-minded, the other staid and responsible. Yet Abigail had loved them both.

When she was being brutally honest with herself, she could admit *that* was at least part of the reason for her natural reserve with Anna Galvez—small-minded, petty jealousy.

A weird kind of sibling rivalry, even.

Abigail had loved Anna—enough to leave her half of Brambleberry House and all its contents. Sage knew she was being selfish but she couldn't help resenting it. Not the house—she couldn't care less about that—but Abigail's affection.

"I'd better get going," Sage said.

"Uh, would you like a ride since we're both going the same way?"

She shook her head. "I'm good. Thanks anyway. If you give me a ride, I won't be able to come home at lunch."

"Oh. Right. I'll see you later then."

Sage stuffed her bag in the wicker basket of her one-speed bike and headed off to town. A moment later, Anna pulled past in her white minivan, moving at a cautious speed on the curving road.

Sage knew the roomy van was a practical choice since Anna probably had to transport things for the store, but she couldn't help thinking how the vehicle seemed to perfectly mirror Anna's personality: bland and businesslike and boring.

Somebody had certainly climbed out of bed on the bitchy side, she chided herself, resolving that she would think only pleasant thoughts about Anna Galvez today, if she thought of her at all.

The same went for little sea sprites she had met on the beach and their entirely too-gorgeous fathers. She had too much to do today with all the chaos and confusion of her first day of camp to spend time thinking about Chloe and Eben Spencer.

The road roughly followed the shore here. Through the heavy pines, she could catch a glimpse of the sea stacks and hear the low murmur of the waves. Three houses down, she waved at a neighbor pulling out of his driveway in a large pickup truck with Garrett Carpentry on the side.

He was heading the other direction toward Manzanita but Will Garrett pulled up alongside her and rolled down his passenger-side window. "Morning, Sage."

She straddled her bike. "Hey, Will."

"Sorry I haven't made it over to look at the work you want done on the house. Been a busy week."

She stared. "Work? What work?"

"Anna called me last week. Said she wanted me to give her a bid for a possible remodel of the kitchen and bathroom on the second-floor apartment. She also wanted me to check the feasibility of knocking out a couple walls in Abigail's apartment to open up the floor plan a little."

"Oh, did she?"

Anger swept over her, hot and bright. Any warmth she might have been trying to force herself into feeling toward Anna seeped out into the dirt.

How dare she?

They had agreed to discuss any matters pertaining to the house and come to a consensus on them, but Anna hadn't said a single word about any of this.

Abigail had left the house to both of them, which meant they *both* should make minor little decisions like knocking out walls and remodeling kitchens. Yet Anna hadn't bothered to bring this up, even when they were talking a few moments ago.

Was her opinion so insignificant?

She knew her anger was overblown—irrational, even—but she couldn't help it. It was too soon. She wasn't ready to go knocking down walls and remodeling kitchens, erasing any sign of the crumbling old house Abigail had loved so dearly.

"She didn't talk to you about it?"

"Not yet," she said grimly.

Something in her tone of voice—or maybe the smoke curling out of her ears—had tipped him off that she wasn't pleased. His expression turned wary. "Well, uh, if you talk to her, let her know I'm going to try to come by this evening to check things out, if that's still okay. Seven or so. One of you can give me a buzz if that's a problem."

He looked eager to escape. She sighed—she shouldn't vent her frustration on Will. It certainly wasn't his fault Anna Galvez was a bossy, managing, stiff-necked pencil-pusher who seemed to believe she knew what was best for the whole bloody world.

She forced a smile. "I'm sure it will be fine. See you tonight."

Though he didn't smile in return—Will rarely smiled anymore—he nodded and put his truck in gear, then headed down the road.

She watched after him for only a moment, then continued pedaling her way toward town.

She still simmered with anger toward Anna's high-handedness, but it was tempered by her usual ache of sorrow for Will. So much pain in the world. Sometimes she couldn't bear it.

She tried her best to leave the world a better place than when she found it. But riding a bike to work and volunteering with Meals on Wheels seemed exercises in futility when she couldn't do a darn thing to ease the burden of those she cared about.

Will was another of Abigail's lost sheep—Sage's affectionate term for the little band of creatures her friend had watched over with her endless supply of love. Abigail seemed to collect people in need and gathered them toward her. The lonely, the forgotten, the grieving. Will had been right there with the rest of them.

No, that wasn't exactly true. Will had belonged to Abigail long before he had ever needed watching over. He had grown up in the same house where he now lived and he and his wife Robin had both known and loved Abigail all their lives.

Sage had lived at Brambleberry House long enough to remember him when he was a handsome charmer, with a teasing grin for everyone. He used to charge into Abigail's parlor and sweep her off her feet, twirling her around and around.

He always had a funny story to tell and he had invariably been the first one on the scene whenever anyone needed help—whether it was moving a piano or spreading a dump-truckload of gravel on a driveway or pumping out a flooded basement.

When Sage moved in upstairs at Brambleberry, Will had become like a big brother to her, offering her the same warm affection he poured out on everyone else in town. Robin had been just as bighearted—lovely and generous and open.

When Robin discovered Sage didn't having a dining room table yet, she had put her husband to work on one and Will had crafted a beautiful round piece of art as a housewarming present.

Sage had soaked it all in, had reveled in the miracle that she had finally found a place to belong among these wonderful people who had opened their lives to her.

If Abigail had been the heart of her circle of friends, Will had been the sturdy, reliable backbone and Robin the nerve center. Their little pigtailed toddler Cara had just been everyone's joy.

Then in the blink of an eye, everything changed.

So much pain.

She let out a breath as she gave a hand signal and turned onto the street toward work. Robin and Will had been crazy about each other. She had walked in on them once in a corner of Abigail's yard at a Fourth of July barbecue. They hadn't been kissing, had just been holding each other, but even from several yards away Sage could feel the love vibrating between them, a strong, tangible connection.

She couldn't imagine the depth of Will's pain at knowing that kind of love and losing it.

Oddly, the mental meanderings made her think of Eben Spencer, sweet little Chloe's abrupt, unfriendly father. The girl had said her mother was dead. Did Eben mourn her loss as deeply as Will did Robin and little Cara, killed two years ago by a drunk driver as they were walking across the street not far from here?

She pulled up to the center and looped her bike lock through the rack out front, determined to put Eben and Chloe Spencer out of her head.

She didn't want to think about either of them. She had learned early in her time at Cannon Beach not to pay much mind to the tourists. Like the fragile summer, they disappeared too soon.

Her resolve was tested even before lunchtime. Since the weather held through the morning, she and her dozen new campers gathered at a picnic table under the spreading boughs of a pine tree outside the center.

She was showing them intertidal zone specimens in aquarium display cases collected earlier that morning by center staffers when she heard a familiar voice call her name.

She turned to find her new friend from the morning barreling toward her, eyes wide, her gamine face animated.

Moving at a slower pace came Eben Spencer, his silk, undoubtedly expensive tie off-center and his hair slightly messed. He did *not* look as if he were having a great day.

Of course, when Sage was having a lousy day, she ended up with circles under her eyes, stress lines cutting through her face and a pounding headache she could swear was visible for miles around.

Eben Spencer just looked slightly rumpled in an entirely too-sexy way.

Heedless of the other children in the class, Chloe rushed to her and threw her arms around Sage's waist.

"It's not my fault this time, I promise."

Under other circumstances, she might have been annoyed at the interruption to her class but she couldn't ignore Chloe's distress—or the frustration stamped on Eben's features.

"Lindsey, can you take over for a minute?" she asked her assistant camp director.

"Of course." The college student who had worked for the nature center every summer since high school stepped forward and Sage led Eben and Chloe away from the interested campers.

"What's not your fault? What's going on?"

"I didn't do *anything*, I swear. It's not my fault at *all* that she was so mean."

Sage looked to Eben for elucidation.

"The caregiver the agency in Portland sent over was…unacceptable." Eben raked a hand through his wavy hair, messing it even more.

"She was mean to me," Chloe said. "She wouldn't let me walk out to the beach, even when I told her my dad said it was okay. She didn't believe me so I called my dad and she got mad at me and pulled my hair and said I was a bad word."

From that explanation, she gathered the caregiver hadn't appreciated an eight-year-old going over her head.

"Oh, dear. A bad word, huh?"

Chloe nodded. "She called me a spoiled little poop, only she didn't say poop."

"I'm sorry," Sage said, trying to figure out exactly what part she played in this unfolding drama.

"I didn't care about the name but I didn't like that she pulled my hair. She didn't have to be so mean. I think she was a *big* poop."

"Chloe," Her father said sternly.

"Well, I do. So I called my dad again and told him what she did and he came right over from The Sea Urchin and told her to leave right now. He said a bad word, too, but I think she deserved it."

She gave a quick glance at her father, then mouthed H-E-L-L.

Sage had to fight a smile. "I see," she said. She found it admirably unexpected that Eben would rush to his daughter's defense.

"And now the place that sent her doesn't have anybody else to take care of me."

Sage raised her eyebrows and glanced at Eben. "I suppose the temp pool is probably pretty shallow right now since the tourist season is heading into full gear."

"I'm figuring that out," he answered. "The agency says it will be at least tomorrow or the next day before they can find someone else. In the meantime, I've got conference calls scheduled all day."

Sage waited to hear what all of this had to do with her, though she was beginning to guess. Her speculation was confirmed by his next words.

"I can't expect Chloe to entertain herself in a strange place while I'm occupied. I remembered you mentioning a summer camp and hoped that you might have room for one more."

"Oh, I'm sorry. We're completely full."

The center had always maintained a strict limit of twelve campers per session to ensure an adequate adult-to-student ratio. Beyond that, she had her hands full this year. Three of the children had learning disabilities and she had already figured out after the first few hours that two more might be on their way to becoming behavior problems if she couldn't figure out how to channel their energy.

Even as she thought of the trouble to her staff if she added another camper, her mind raced trying to figure out how to accommodate Eben and his daughter.

"I was afraid you would say that." He smiled stiffly. "Thank you for your time anyway. We'll try to figure something else out."

He looked resigned but accepting. His daughter, on the other hand, appeared close to tears. Her shoulders slumped and her chin quivered.

"But I really wanted to come to camp with Sage," she wailed. "It sounded super, super fun! I don't want to stay in a boring house all day long while you talk on the phone!"

"Chloe, that's enough. If the camp doesn't have room for you, that's the way it is."

"You think I'm a little poop, too, don't you?" Chloe's chin was definitely quivering now. "That's why you don't want me in your camp. You don't like me, either."

"Oh, honey, that's not true. We just have rules about how many children we can have in our camp."

"I would be really good. You wouldn't even know I'm here. Oh, please, Sage!"

She studied them both—Chloe so dejected and her father resigned. She had to wonder how much pride he had forced himself to swallow for his daughter's sake to bring her here and ask Sage for a favor.

How could she disappoint them?

"We're at capacity," she finally said, "but I think we can probably find room to squeeze in one more."

"You mean it? Really?" The girl looked afraid to hope.

Sage nodded and Chloe squealed with delight and hugged her again. "Yes! Thank you, thank you, thank you!"

Sage hugged her in return. "You're welcome. You're going to have to work hard and listen to me and the other grown-ups, though."

"I will. I'll be super super good."

Sage glanced up to meet Eben's gaze and found him watching her with that same odd, slightly thunderstruck expression she had seen him wear earlier that morning.

She didn't fathom it—nor did she quite understand why it made her insides tremble.

"I'm busy with the class out here," she spoke briskly to hide her reaction, "but if you go inside the center, Amy can provide you with the registration information. Tell her I said we could make an exception this once and add one more camper beyond our usual limit."

"Thank you, Ms. Benedetto." One corner of his mouth lifted into a relieved smile and the trembling in her stomach seemed to go into hyperdrive, much like the Harder twins after a little sugar.

Somehow that slight smile made him look even more attractive and her reaction to it alarmed her.

"Amy will give you a list of supplies you will need to provide for Chloe." Annoyance at herself sharpened her voice. "She's going to need waterproof boots and a warmer jacket this afternoon when we go out to Haystack, though we can probably scrounge something for her today."

"Thank you."

"May I go with the other children?" Chloe asked, her green eyes gleaming with eagerness.

"Sure," Sage said. She and Eben watched Chloe race to the picnic table and squeeze into a spot between two girls of similar ages, who slid over to make room for her.

She turned back to Eben. "Our class ends at four, whether your conference calls are done or not."

He sent her a swift look. "I'll be sure to hang up on my attorneys if they run long. I wouldn't want to keep you waiting."

"It's not me you would be letting down. It's Chloe."

His mouth tightened with clear irritation but she watched in fascination as he carefully pushed it away and resumed a polite expression. "Thank you again for accommodating Chloe. I know you're stretching the rules for her and I do appreciate it."

Without waiting for an answer, he turned around and walked toward the center. She watched him go, that fast, take-no-prisoners stride eating up the beach.

What a disagreeable man. He ought to have a British accent for all the stuffy reserve in his voice.

She sighed. Too bad he had to be gorgeous. Someone with his uptight personality ought to have the looks to match, tight, thin lips, a honker of a nose, and squinty pale eyes set too close together.

Instead, Eben Spencer had been blessed with stunning green eyes, wavy dark hair and lean, chiseled features.

Didn't matter, she told herself. In her book, personality mattered far more than looks and by all indications Eben Spencer scored a big fat zero in that department.

"Ms. B, Ms. B.! What's this one? Lindsey doesn't know."

She turned back to the picnic table. She had work to do, she reminded herself sternly. She needed to keep her attention tightly focused on her day camp and the thirteen children in it—not on particularly gorgeous hotel magnates with all the charm of a spiny urchin.

Chapter Three

"**Y**our daughter will just *love* the day camp." The bubbly receptionist inside the office delivered a thousand-watt smile out of white teeth in perfect alignment as she handed him the papers.

"It's one of our most popular summer activities," she went on. "People come from all over to bring their children to learn about the rocky shore and the kids just eat it up. And our camp director is just wonderful. The children all adore her. Sometimes I think she's just a big kid herself."

He raised an eyebrow, his mind on Sage Benedetto, and her honey-blond curls, lush curves and all that blatant sensuality.

"Is that right?" he murmured.

The receptionist either didn't catch his dry tone or chose to ignore him. He voted for the former.

"You should see her when they're tide-pooling, in her big old boots and a grin as big as the Haystack. Sage knows everything about the coastal ecosystem. She can identify every creature in a tide pool in an instant and can tell you what they eat, how they reproduce and who their biggest predator might be. She's just amazing."

He didn't want to hear the receptionist gush about Sage Benedetto. He really preferred to know as little about her as possible. He had already spent the morning trying to shake thoughts of her out of his head so he could focus on business.

He smiled politely. "That's good to hear. I'm relieved Chloe will be in competent hands."

"Oh, you won't find better hands anywhere on the coast, I promise," she assured him.

For a brief second, he had a wickedly inappropriate reaction to that bit of information, but with determined effort, he managed to channel his attention back to the registration papers in front of them.

He quickly read over and signed every document required—just a little more paperwork than he usually faced when purchasing a new hotel.

He didn't mind the somewhat exorbitant fee or the tacked-on late-registration penalty. If not for Sage and her summer camp, his options would have been severely limited.

He didn't have high hopes that the agency in Portland

would find someone quickly, which would probably mean he would have to cancel the entire trip and abandon the conference calls scheduled for the week or fly in his assistant to keep an eye on Chloe, something neither Chloe nor Betsy would appreciate.

No, Sage Benedetto had quite likely saved a deal that was fiercely important to Spencer Hotels.

He would have liked to surrender Chloe to someone a little more…restrained…but he wasn't going to quibble.

"All right. She's all set, registered for the entire week. Now, you know you're going to need to provide your daughter with a pair of muck boots and rain-gear, right?"

"Ms. Benedetto already informed me of that. I'll be sure Chloe is equipped with everything she needs tomorrow."

"Here's the rest of the list of what you need."

"Thank you."

He took it from her with a quick glance at his watch. He was supposed to be talking to his advertising team in New York in twenty minutes and he wasn't sure he was going to make it.

Outside, steely clouds had begun to gather with the capriciousness of seaside weather. Even with them, the view was stunning, with dramatic sea stacks offshore and a wide sandy beach that seemed to stretch for miles.

He shifted his gaze to the group of children still gathered around the picnic table. Chloe looked as if she had settled right in. As she chattered to one of the other girls, her eyes were bright and happy in a way he hadn't seen in a long time.

He was vastly relieved, grateful to see her natural energy directed toward something educational and fun instead of toward getting into as much trouble as humanly possible for an eight-year-old girl.

This next few days promised to be difficult with all the new conditions Stanley Wu was imposing on the sale of his hotel. Having a good place for Chloe to go during the day would ease his path considerably.

His attention twisted to the woman standing at the head of the table. In khaki slacks and a navy-blue knit shirt, Sage Benedetto should have looked stern and official. But she was laughing at something one of the children said, her blond curls escaping a loose braid.

With her olive-toned skin and blonde hair, she looked exotic and sensual. Raw desire tightened his gut but he forced himself to ignore it as he walked the short distance to the cluster of children.

Chloe barely looked up when he approached. "I'm leaving," he told her. "I'll be back this afternoon to pick you up."

"Okay. Bye, Daddy," she chirped, then immediately turned her attention back to the other girls and their activity as if she had already forgotten his presence.

He stood by the table for a moment, feeling awkward and wishing he were better at this whole parenting thing. His love for his daughter was as vast and tumultuous as the ocean and most of the time it scared the hell out of him.

He looked up and found Sage watching him, a warmth in her eyes that hadn't been there earlier. Sunlight slanted beneath the clouds, turning the hair escaping her braid to a riotous halo of curls around her face.

She looked like something from an old master painting, lush and earthy, and when her features lightened into a smile, lust tightened inside him again.

"Don't worry, Mr. Spencer. We'll take good care of Chloe."

He nodded, angry again at this instinctive reaction to her. The only thing for it was to leave the situation, he decided, to avoid contact with her as much as possible.

"I have no doubts you will. Excuse me. I've got to return to work."

At his abrupt tone, the warmth slid away from her features. "Right. Your empire-building awaits."

He almost preferred her light mockery to that momentary flicker of warmth. It certainly made it easier for him to keep his inappropriate responses under control.

"I'll be back for Chloe at four."

He started to walk away, then paused, feeling churlish and ungrateful. She was doing him a huge favor and he couldn't return that favor with curt rudeness.

"Uh, thank you again for finding space for her. I appreciate it."

Her smile was much cooler this time. "I have no doubts you do," she murmured.

He studied her for a moment, then matched the temperature of his own smile to hers and walked to the nature center's parking lot where his rented Jaguar waited.

His mind was still on Sage Benedetto as he drove

through town, stopping at a crosswalk for a trio of gray-haired shoppers to make their slow way across the road, then two mothers pushing strollers.

He forced himself to curb his impatience as he waited. Even though it was early June, the tourist season on the Oregon Coast seemed to be in full swing, something that boded favorably for someone in the hotel business.

He had learned that the season never really ended here, unlike some other resort areas. There was certainly a high season and a low season but people came to the coast year-round.

In the summer, families came to play in the sand and enjoy the natural beauty; winter brought storm watchers and beachcombers to the wide public beaches.

Though his ultimate destination was his temporary quarters, he automatically slowed as he approached The Sea Urchin. He could see it set back among Sitka spruce and pine: the graceful, elegant architecture, the weathered gray-stone facade, the extravagant flower gardens already blooming with vibrant color.

He wanted it, as he hadn't coveted anything in a long, long time. In the four months since he had first seen the hotel on a trip down the coast to scout possible property locations, he had become obsessed with owning it.

His original plan had been to build a new hotel somewhere along the coast, possibly farther south in the Newport area.

But the moment he caught sight of The Sea Urchin—

and Cannon Beach—the place called to him in a way he couldn't begin to explain.

He had no idea why it affected him so strongly. He wasn't one for capricious business moves, heaven knows. In the dozen years since he'd taken over his family company at the ripe age of twenty-four, he had tried to make each decision with a cool head and a sharp eye for the bottom line.

Building a new property made better business sense—everything was custom designed and there were more modern amenities. That would have been a far more lucrative choice for Spencer Hotels and was the option his people had been pushing.

But when he saw The Sea Urchin, with its clean lines and incredible views of the coast, his much-vaunted business acumen seemed to drift away with the tide.

It had been rainy and dismal that February day, a cold, dank wind whistling off the Pacific. He had been calling himself all kinds of fool for coming here in the first place, for packing his schedule so tightly when he was supposed to be leaving for the United Kingdom in only a few days.

But on the recommendation of a local woman, he had driven past The Sea Urchin and seen it silhouetted against the sea, warm, welcoming lights in all the windows, and he had wanted it.

He had never known this sense of *rightness* before, but somehow he couldn't shake the odd sense that he could make this small hotel with its twenty guest rooms the glimmering crown jewel of Spencer Hotels.

He sighed and forced himself to drive past the hotel. *He* might be certain his destiny and The Sea Urchin's were somehow intertwined, but Stanley and Jade Wu were proving a little harder to convince.

Renewed frustration simmered through him. A week ago, this sale was supposed to be a done deal. All the parties involved had finally agreed on an asking price—a quarter million dollars more than Eben had planned to pay when he and the Wus first discussed the sale in February.

He thought all the legalities had been worked out with his advance team before he flew to Portland. The only thing left was for Stanley and Jade to sign the papers, but they had been putting him off for two days.

He could feel the property slipping through his fingers and for the first time in his business life, he didn't know how the hell to grab hold of something he wanted.

He understood their ambivalence. They had run The Sea Urchin for thirty-five years, had built it through skill and hard work and shrewd business sense into a stylishly beautiful hotel. Surrendering the family business to a stranger—seeing it folded into the *empire* Sage Benedetto had mocked with such disdain—could only be difficult for them.

He understood all that, Eben thought again as he pulled into the driveway and climbed out of the car, but his patience was trickling away rapidly.

He fiercely wanted The Sea Urchin and he wasn't sure how he would cope with his disappointment if the deal fell through. And in the meantime, he still had a company of a hundred hotels to run.

Oh, she was tired.

Right now the idea of sliding into a hot bath with a good book sounded like a slice of heaven. In the gathering twilight, Sage pedaled home with a steady drizzle soaking her to the skin.

So much for the weather forecasters' prediction of sunshine for the next three days. Having lived in Oregon for five years now, she ought to know better. The weather was fickle and erratic. She had learned to live with it and even enjoyed it for the most part.

She tried to always be prepared for any eventuality. Of course, this was the day she had forgotten to pack her rain slicker in her bike basket.

She blamed her negligence on her distraction that morning with Eben and Chloe Spencer, though maybe that was only because she was approaching their beach house.

She wiped rain out of her eyes as she passed it. A sleek silver Jaguar was sprawled arrogantly in the driveway.

Of course. What else would she expect?

Against her will, her eyes were drawn to the wide bay window in front. The blinds were open and she thought she saw a dark shadow move around inside before she quickly jerked her attention back to the road.

Wouldn't it be just like her to have a wipeout right in front of his house, with him watching out the window?

She stubbornly worked to put them both out of her

head as she rode the half mile to Brambleberry House. The house came into view as she rounded the last corner and some of her exhaustion faded away in the sweet, welcome comfort of coming home.

She loved this old place with its turrets and gables and graceful old personality, though some of the usual joy she felt returning to it had been missing since Abigail's death.

As she pedaled into the driveway, Conan barked a halfhearted greeting from the front porch.

Stubborn thing. He should be waiting inside where it was warm and dry. Instead, he insisted on waiting on the front porch—for her or for Anna or for Abigail, she didn't know. She got the sense Conan kept expecting Abigail to drive her big Buick home any moment now.

Conan loped out into the rain to greet her by the fence and she ached at the sadness in his big eyes. "Let me put my bike away, okay? Then you can tell me about your day while I change into dry clothes."

She opened the garage door and as she parked her bike, she heard Conan bark again and the sound of a vehicle outside. She glanced out the wide garage door to see Will Garrett's pickup truck pulling into the driveway.

Rats. She'd forgotten all about their conversation that morning. So much for her dreams of a long soak.

He climbed out into the rain—though he was at least smart enough to wear a Gore-Tex jacket.

"Hi Will. Anna's not here yet."

"I'm sure she'll be here soon. I'm a little early."

"I never told her you were coming. I'm sorry, Will. I knew there was something I forgot to do today. I honestly don't have any idea when she'll be home."

The man she had met five years ago when she first moved here would have grinned and teased her about her bubbleheaded moment. But the solemn stranger he had become since the death of his wife and baby girl only nodded. "I can come back later. Not a problem."

Guilt was a miserable companion on a rainy night. "No. Come in. You're here, you might as well get started, at least in the empty apartment. Without Anna here, I don't feel right about taking you into Abigail's apartment to see what to do there, since it's her territory now. But I have a key to the second floor. I just need to run up and get it."

"Better change into something dry while you're up there. Wouldn't do for you to catch pneumonia."

His solemn concern absurdly made her want to cry. She hadn't had anybody to fuss over her since Abigail's death.

"I'll hurry," she assured him, and dripped her way up the stairs, leaving him behind with Conan.

She returned five minutes later in dry jeans, a sweat-shirt and toweled-dry hair. She hurried down the stairs to the second-floor landing, where Will must have climbed with Conan. The two of them sat on the top step and the dog had his chin on Will's knee.

"Sorry to leave you waiting." She pulled out a key and fitted it in the keyhole.

Will rose. "Not a problem. Conan's been telling me about his day."

"He's quite the uncanny conversationalist, isn't he?"

He managed half a smile and followed her into the apartment.

The rooms here, their furnishings blanketed in dust covers, had a vaguely forlorn feeling to them. Unlike the rest of the house, the air was stale and close. Whenever she came in here, Sage thought the apartment seemed to be waiting for something, silly as that seemed.

Abigail had rented the second floor only twice in the five years Sage had lived at Brambleberry House. Each time had been on a temporary basis, the apartment becoming a transitional home for Abigail's strays for just a few months at a time.

The place should be lived in. It was comfortable and roomy, with three bedrooms, a huge living room and a fairly good-sized kitchen.

The plumbing was in terrible shape and the vinyl tiles in the kitchen and bathroom was peeling and outdated, in definite need of replacement. The appliances and cabinets in the kitchen were ancient, too, and the whole place could use new paint and some repairs to the crumbling lathe and plaster walls.

Despite the battle scars, the apartment had big windows all around that let light throughout the rooms and the living room enjoyed a particularly breathtaking view of the sea. Not as nice as the one from her third-floor apartment, but lovely still.

She wandered to the window now and realized she

had a perfect view of Eben and Chloe Spencer's place, the lights still beating back the darkness.

"Hey Sage, can you come hold the end of the tape measure?"

She jerked out of her reverie and followed his voice to the bathroom. For the next few minutes she assisted while Will studied, measured, measured again and finally jotted figures on his clipboard.

They were in the kitchen when through the open doorway she saw Conan suddenly lift his head from his morose study of the peeling wallpaper. A moment later, she heard the squeak of the front door and reminded herself to add WD-40 to her shopping list.

Conan scrambled up, nosed open the door and galloped for the stairs. A moment later he was back, with Anna not far behind him.

"Hey, Will. I saw your van out front. I didn't realize you were coming tonight."

Sage fought down her guilt. She wasn't the one in the wrong here. Anna had no business arranging all this without talking to her.

"I meant to call you but the day slipped away from me," she said. "I bumped into Will this morning on the way to work and he told me he was coming out tonight to give us a bid on the work we apparently want him to do."

Anna didn't miss her tight tone. Sage thought she saw color creep over her dusky cheekbones. "I figured there was no harm having him come out to take a look. Information is always a good thing. We need to know what our initial capital outlay might be to renovate the apartment so we can accurately determine whether it's cost-effective to rent it out."

Sage really hated that prim, businessy tone. Did any personality at all lurk under Anna's stiff facade? It had to. She knew it must. Abigail had cared about her, had respected her enough to sell her the gift shop and to leave her half of Brambleberry House.

Sage had seen little sign of it, though. She figured Anna probably fell asleep at night dreaming of her portfolio allocation.

She didn't want to battle this out tonight. She was too darn tired after wrestling thirteen energetic kids all day.

Instead, she reached into her pocket for the dog treat she had grabbed upstairs when she had changed her clothes. She palmed it and held it casually at thigh level.

Conan was a sucker for the bacon treats. Just as she intended, the dog instantly left Anna's side and sidled over to her. Anna tried to hide her quick flicker of hurt but she wasn't quite quick enough.

"Dirty trick," Will murmured from behind her.

Having a witness to her sneakiness made her feel petty and small. She wasn't fit company for anyone tonight. She let out a breath and resolved to try harder to be kind.

"I think we're done up here," Will said. "Should I take a look at the first floor now?"

Anna nodded and led the way down the stairs. Sage thought about escaping to her apartment and indulging in that warm bath that had been calling her name all evening, but she knew it would be cowardly, especially after Will had witnessed her subversive bribery of Conan.

She followed them down the stairs to Abigail's apartment. With some trepidation, Sage stood in the doorway. She hadn't been here since Anna moved her things in two weeks ago. She couldn't help expecting to see Abigail bustle out of the kitchen with her tea tray and a plateful of Pepperidge Farm Raspberry Milanos.

All three of them—four, counting Conan—paused inside the living room. Shared grief for the woman they had all loved twisted around them like thorny vines.

Anna was the first to break the charged moment as she briskly moved into the room. "Sorry about the mess. If I'd had warning, I might have had time to straighten up a little."

Sage couldn't see much mess, just a newspaper spread out on the coffee table and a blanket jumbled in a heap on the couch, but she figured those few items slightly out of place probably affected Anna as much as if a hurricane had blown through.

"What I would like to do is knock down the wall between the kitchen and the dining room to make the kitchen bigger. And then I was wondering about the feasibility of taking out the wall between the two smaller bedrooms to make that a big master."

Abigail's presence was so strong here. While Will and Anna were busy in the kitchen, Sage stood in the middle of the living room and closed her eyes, her throat tight. She could still smell her here, that soft scent of freesia.

Abigail wouldn't have wanted her to wallow in this wrenching grief, she knew, but she couldn't seem to fight it back.

For one odd second, the scent of freesia seemed stronger and she could swear she felt a soft, papery hand on her cheek.

To distract herself from the weird sensation, she glanced around the rooms and through the open doorway to one of the bedrooms and suddenly caught sight of Abigail's vast doll collection.

Collecting dolls had always seemed too ordinary a hobby for Abigail, given her friend's other eccentricities, but Abigail had loved each piece in the room.

She moved to the doorway and flipped on the light switch, enjoying as always that first burst of amazement at the floor-to-ceiling display cases crammed full of thousands of dolls. There was her favorite, a mischievous-looking senior citizen wearing a tie-dyed shirt and a peace medallion. Golden Flower Child. She was certain the artist had handcrafted it specifically for Abigail.

"You should take some of them up to your apartment."

Sage quickly dropped her hand from the doll's familiar smile to find Anna watching her.

"They're part of the contents of the house, which she left jointly to both of us," Anna went on. "Half of them are yours."

She glanced at the aging hippie doll with longing,

then shook her head. "They belong together. I'm not sure we should split up the collection."

After a long pause, Anna's expression turned serious. "Why don't you take them all upstairs with you, then?"

She had a feeling the offer had not been an easy one for Anna to make. It touched her somewhere deep inside. The lump in her throat swelled and she felt even more guilty for the dog-treat trick.

"We don't have to decide anything like that today. For now, we can leave them where they are, as long as you don't mind."

Before Anna could voice the arguments Sage could see brewing in her dark eyes, Will joined them. "You want the good news or the bad?"

"Good news," Anna said instantly. Sage would have saved the best for last. Good news after bad always made the worst seem a little more palatable.

"None of the walls you want to take out are weight-bearing, so we should be okay that way."

"What's the bad?" Anna asked.

"We're going to have to reroute some plumbing. It's going to cost you."

He gave a figure that staggered Sage, though Anna didn't seem at all surprised.

"Well, there's no rush on this floor. What about the work upstairs?"

Those figures were no less stunning. "That's more than reasonable," Anna said. "Are you positive that will cover your entire overhead? I don't want you skimping your profit."

"It's fair."

Anna gave him a careful look, then smiled. "It *will* be fair when we tack back on the twenty percent you cut off the labor costs."

"I give my friends a deal."

"Not these friends. We'll pay your going rate or we'll find somebody else to do the work."

Anna's insistence surprised Sage as much as the numbers. She would have expected the other woman to pinch pennies wherever she could and she had to admit she was impressed that she refused to take advantage of Will's generosity.

"You'll take a discount and that's final," he said firmly. "You'll never find another contractor who will treat Brambleberry House with the same loving care."

"You guys can hash this out better without me," Sage announced. She wasn't sure she could spend any more time in Abigail's apartment without breaking into tears. "I'm tired and I'm hungry. Right now all I want to do is fix some dinner and take a long, hot soak in the tub with a glass of wine. You can give me the details tomorrow."

"I'll walk Conan tonight. It's my turn," Anna said.

She nodded her agreement and headed up the stairs to her veggie burger and silence.

Chapter Four

This was the reason he wanted The Sea Urchin so desperately.

Eben leaned his elbows on the deck railing off the back of their beach house watching dawn spread out across the Pacific the next morning, fingers of pink and lavender and orange slicing through the wisps of fog left from the rains of the night before.

The air smelled of the sea, salty and sharp; gulls wheeled and dived looking for breakfast.

He was the only human in sight—a rare occurrence for him. He wasn't used to solitude and quiet, not with chattering Chloe around all the time. He wasn't completely sure he liked it—but he knew that if he could package this kind of morning for all his properties, Spencer Hotels would never have a vacancy again.

Normal people—people very much unlike uptight Californian businessmen—would eat this whole relaxation thing up. The Sea Urchin would be busy year-round, with people booking their suites months, even years, in advance.

He sipped his coffee and tried to force the tension from his shoulders. Another few days of this and he would be a certifiable beach bum, ready to chuck the stress of life in San Francisco for a quiet stretch of shoreline and a good cup of coffee.

Or maybe not.

He had never been one to sit still for long, not with so much to do. He'd been up since four taking a conference call with Tokyo in preparation for a series of meetings there next week and in two hours he would have to drive the ninety minutes to Portland to meet with his attorneys.

Despite the calm and beauty of the morning, his mind raced with his lengthy to-do list.

In the distance he saw a jogger running up the beach toward town and envy poked him. He would give his coffee and a whole lot more to be the one running along the hard-packed sand close to the surf, working off these restless edges.

Others found calm and peace in the soothing sound of the sea. For Eben, a good, hard run usually did the trick. But with Chloe asleep inside, that was impossible.

He couldn't leave her alone in a strange place, even if he left a note and took his cell phone so she could reach him.

The jogger drew closer and recognition clicked in at exactly the same moment he heard a bark of greeting. A moment later, Sage Benedetto's big gangly red dog loped into view.

The dog barked again, changed directions and headed straight toward him. After an odd hesitation, the big dog's owner waved briefly and followed her animal.

Though he knew it was foolish, anticipation curled through him like those tendrils of fog on the water.

She was still some distance away when the dog nuzzled his head under Eben's hand, looking for attention. He had never had a pet and wasn't very used to animals, but he scratched the dog's chin and was rewarded by the dog nudging his hand for more.

When Sage approached, he saw she was wearing bike shorts and a hooded sweatshirt with an emblem that read Portland Saturday Market across the front.

She looked soft and sensual in the early morning light, like some kind of lush fertility goddess. Her exotic features were flushed and her hair was in a wild ponytail.

She looked as if she had just climbed out of bed after making love all night long.

His insides burned with sudden hunger but he hid his reaction behind a casual smile. "Great morning for a run."

She raised an eyebrow. "You think?"

"I was just now pondering how much I'd love to be

out there doing the same thing if only Chloe weren't asleep inside."

She gave a sudden delighted smile that made him feel as if the sun had just climbed directly above his beach house. Before he could catch his breath, she grabbed the coffee mug straight out of his hand and sipped it, pressing her mouth exactly where his own lips had been.

"Problem solved. I'll stay here in case Chloe wakes up and you can take Conan."

She made a shooing gesture with the hand not holding his coffee. "You two boys go on and run to your little hearts' content and I'll go back to sleep for a few moments."

She slid into one of the wide, plump rockers on the deck and closed her eyes, his mug still cradled in her hands.

She was completely serious, Eben realized, not quite sure whether to be amused or annoyed. But with a sudden anticipation zinging through him, he couldn't help but smile. "At least come inside where it's warm while I throw on some jogging shoes."

She opened her eyes and her gaze flashed down to his bare toes then back at him with an inscrutable expression on her features. "I'm fine out here, but if you would feel better having me inside in case Chloe wakes up, I have no problem with that, either."

She followed him inside to the living room with its floor-to-ceiling windows overlooking the shore.

"Nice," she murmured.

He was intensely aware of her, more than he had been of any woman in a long, long time.

He was also cognizant of the fact that they were virtually alone, with only his daughter sleeping on the other side of the house, something he *didn't* want to think about.

"Give me five minutes to grab my shoes."

She was already nestling into the comfortable leather couch that faced the windows, her eyes already closing, her muscles going slack. "No problem. Take your time. This is perfect. Absolutely perfect."

He threw on his shoes quickly and hurried back to the family room. She gave all appearances of being asleep. He watched her for only a moment, entranced by the wisp of honey-colored hair curling over her cheekbone.

When he realized he was gazing at her like some kind of Peeping Tom, he hurried out the door to the deck and whistled to Conan, who was busy marking every support of the deck.

The dog stopped mid-pee, barked with an eagerness that matched Eben's and the two of them set off down the beach.

With a sense of freedom he hadn't known in a long time, he ran on the hard-packed sand, dodging waves and the occasional long, ragged clump of kelp. The dog raced right along with him, easily matching his stride to Eben's and in no time they had a comfortable rhythm.

By the time they reached the headlands on the north end of the beach, he felt loose and liberated, as if the jog had chased all the cobwebs from his mind.

He paused for a moment to enjoy the full splendor of the sunrise slanting out across the water while the dog chased a couple of seagulls pecking at something in the sand.

After some time, Eben checked his watch with some regret. "We'd better hustle back. Some of us need to go to work," he told the dog, who tilted his head with a quizzical look then barked as if he understood exactly what Eben had said. The dog turned and charged back down the beach the way they'd come.

The beach had been largely empty on their way north but on the run back, they passed several other joggers and beachcombers, all of whom greeted him with friendly smiles—or at least offered smiles to Conan.

Several called the dog by name and gave them curious looks that Eben deflected with a wave. All the locals were probably wondering who was running with Sage Benedetto's dog but he didn't have the breath to enlighten any of them, even if he'd wanted to.

"Wait out here," he ordered the sandy dog when they reached the beach house, his breath still coming fast and hard. Conan flopped onto the deck and curled his head in his paws, apparently content to rest.

He let himself into the house and found Sage exactly where he'd left her, sound asleep on his couch.

A quick peek into Chloe's room showed him she was still asleep as well, the blankets jumbled around her feet.

He closed her door with gentle care and returned to

the family room. Okay, so he hadn't worked all the restlessness out of his system, apparently. Some of it still simmered through him, especially as he watched Sage sleep on his couch. She looked rumpled and sexy, her lashes fluttering against the olive skin of her high cheekbones and the slightest of smiles playing over those lush lips.

What was she dreaming about? he wondered, hunger tightening his insides.

Maybe it was a reaction to the blood still pumping through him from the good, hard run—or, he admitted honestly, probably just the delectable woman in front of him—but Eben wanted her more than he could remember ever wanting a woman.

He cleared his throat, again fighting back his heretofore unknown voyeuristic tendencies. "Uh, Ms. Benedetto. Time to go. The run's over."

Her mouth twitched a little in sleep but her eyes remained stubbornly closed. She made a little sleepy sound and rolled over, presenting her back to him, looking for all the world as if she were settling in to nap the morning away.

Now what was he supposed to do?

"Sage?" he said again.

When she still didn't respond, he sighed and reached a hand out to her shoulder. "Sage, wake up. You have to go to work, remember? We both do."

After a moment, she heaved a long sigh and turned over again. She blinked her eyes open and gazed at him in confusion for a moment before he saw consciousness slowly return like the tide coming in.

She sat up, gave a yawn and stretched her arms above her head. Eben swallowed and did his best to remember how to breathe.

"I have to say, that had to be just about the best jog I've had in a month," she murmured with a sleepy, sexy smile.

She rose, stretching again with graceful limbs, and Eben stared at her a long moment—at the becoming flush on her features, at the wild tangle of her hair, at her slightly parted lips.

He sensed exactly the instant his control slipped out the window—when she smiled at him again, her head canted to one side. With a groan, he surrendered the battle and reached for her.

She was soft and warm and smelled of the leather sofa where she had been sleeping and an exotic spicy-sweet flowery scent that had to be purely Sage.

He told himself he would stop with just a tiny taste. He had taken her dog out running, after all. Didn't she owe him something for that? Stealing a little morning kiss seemed like small recompense.

He didn't expect her mouth to taste of coffee and mint and he certainly didn't expect, after one shocked second, for her to make a low, aroused sound in her throat then wrap her arms around his neck as if she couldn't bear the idea of letting him go.

From that point on, he lost all sense of time and

space and reason. His foolish idea of giving into the heat for only an instant with one little taste went out the window along with the rest of his control.

The only thing he could focus on was the woman in his arms—her intoxicating scent and taste, the texture of her sweatshirt under his hands, the soft curves pressing against him.

He needed to stop, for a million reasons. He barely knew the woman. She barely knew him. Chloe could wake and come out of her room any moment. He had just jogged three miles down the beach and back and probably smelled like a locker room.

All these thoughts flickered through his mind but he couldn't quite catch hold of any of them. The blood singing through him and the wild hunger burning up his insides were the only things that seemed to matter.

He deepened the kiss and she sighed against his mouth. He was intensely aware of her soft fingers in his hair, of the other hand curving around his neck. Even with the heat scorching him, the wonder of feeling her hands on him absurdly drew a lump to his throat.

How long had it been since he'd known a woman's touch? Brooke's shockingly sudden death from an aneurysm had been two years ago and he hadn't been with anyone since then. Even for months before her death, things had been rocky between them. He knew he had failed her in many, many ways.

The specter of his disastrous marriage finally helped him regain some small measure of control.

He stilled, then opened his eyes as the sensation of being watched prickled down his spine.

Not Chloe, he hoped, and swept the room with a glance. No, he realized. Sage's big red dog watched them through the wide windows leading to the deck. And if Conan had been human, Eben would have sworn he was grinning at them.

Though he ached at the effort, Eben forced himself to break the kiss and step back, his breathing uneven and his thoughts a tangled mess.

"Well. That was…unexpected," she murmured.

Her color was high but she didn't look upset by their heated embrace, only surprised.

He, on the other hand, was stunned to his core.

What the hell was he thinking? This kind of thing was not at all like him. He was known in all circles—social, business and otherwise—for his cool head and detached calm.

He had spent his life working hard to keep himself in check. Oh, he knew himself well enough to understand it was a survival mechanism from his childhood—if he couldn't control his parents' tumultuous natures, their wild outbursts, their screaming fights, and substance abuse, at least he could contain his own behavior.

Those habits had carried into adulthood and into his marriage. In the heat of anger, Brooke used to call him a machine, accusing him of having no heart, no feeling. She *had* to have an affair, she told him, if only to know what it was like to be with a man who had blood instead of antifreeze running through his veins.

This new, urgent heat for an exotic, wild-haired nature girl sent him way, *way* out of his comfort zone.

"My apologies," he said, his voice stiff. "I'm not quite sure what happened there."

"Aren't you?"

He sent her a swift look and saw the corner of her mouth lift. He didn't like the feeling she was laughing at him.

"You can be certain it won't happen again."

A strange light flickered in the depths of her dark eyes. "Okay. Good to know."

She studied him for a moment, then smiled. He wanted to think the expression looked a little strained but he thought that was possibly his imagination.

"Thank you for taking Conan jogging for me. I admit, I'm not crazy about the whole morning exercise thing. I'm trying to warm up to it but it's been slow going so far. I thought after a month I would enjoy it more, but what are you going to do? It seems to cheer him up a little, though, so I guess I'll stick with it."

He couldn't seem to make his brain work but he managed to catch hold of a few of the pieces of what she said.

"You're telling me your dog is depressed?" he asked, feeling supremely stupid for even posing the question.

"You could say that." She glanced out the window where Conan still watched them and lowered her voice as if the dog could hear them through the glass. "He misses his human companion. She died a month ago."

The dog's *human companion* had died a month ago and Sage had been jogging with Conan for a month. Even in his current disordered state, he figured the two events had to be connected.

"She left you her dog?"

"That and a whole lot of other problems. It's a long story." One she obviously had no intention of sharing with him, he realized as she headed for the door.

"I'd better go. I've got thirteen eager young campers who'll be ready to explore the coastline with me in just an hour. I'm sure you've got things to do, people to see, worlds to conquer and all that."

His mouth tightened at the faint echo of derision in her voice, but before he could defend himself from her obviously harsh view of his life, she opened the door and walked out into the cool morning air, to be greeted with enthusiasm by the dog, who jumped around as if he hadn't seen her in months.

Just now the animal looked far from the bereft, grieving animal she had described. She patted his sides, which had the dog's eyes rolling back ɪn his head. Eben couldn't say he blamed him.

"Thanks again for exercising Conan," she called back.

"No problem. I enjoyed it."

Stepping outside, he decided he wasn't going to think about anything else he might have enjoyed about the morning.

"The run was good for me," he said instead. "Helps keep my brain sharp while I'm swindling retirees and gullible widows out of their life savings."

Her mouth quirked a little at that but she only shook her wild mane of hair and took off down the stairs of his deck and across the beach, the dog close on her heels.

Chapter Five

She tried to tell herself that heated kiss was just a one-shot deal, some weird anomaly of fate and circumstance that would never, ever, *ever* be repeated.

She and Eben were two vastly different people with different values, different tax brackets. Their lives should never have intersected in the first place—and their mouths certainly shouldn't have either.

But as she showered and dressed for work, Sage couldn't shake the odd, jittery feeling that something momentous had just happened to her, something life-changing and substantial.

It was silly, she knew, but she couldn't shake the feeling that her life had just turned a corner down a route she was not at all sure she was prepared to follow.

Just a kiss, she repeated in a stern mantra as she gave Conan one last morning scratch, pulled her bike out of the garage and cycled through the strands of morning fog that hadn't yet burned off. Two people reacting to their unlikely attraction to each other in the usual fashion. One never-to-be-repeated kiss certainly was not about to alter the rest of her life, for heaven's sake.

She was still working hard to convince herself of that when she arrived at the nature center and let herself into her office. She was answering e-mail from a school group interested in arranging a field trip between her camp sessions when Lindsey poked her head into her office.

"So the weirdest thing happened this morning," Lindsey said without preamble.

Sage raised an eyebrow. "Good morning to you, too."

Her assistant director grinned. "Yeah, yeah. Hello, how are you, great to see you and all that. I've been up at the bakery since four already helping my dad so it feels more like lunchtime to me by this time. But back to my weird morning."

She pushed away the lingering memory of Eben and that stunning kiss and tried to focus on Lindsey's story. "Don't tell me you had another creepy dream about old Mr. Delarosa walking down Hemlock Street in a Speedo again."

Lindsey screwed up her face. "No! Ew. Thanks for putting that visual in my head again. I just spent the last three months in intensive therapy trying to purge it."

Sage fought a smile. "Sorry. What happened this morning?"

"I was making the usual morning deliveries of muffins to The Sea Urchin and suddenly this huge dog comes running at me out of nowhere. Scared the bejabbers out of me."

"Yeah?"

"It was Conan, of course."

"Of course. He is the only dog in Cannon Beach, after all."

"Well, maybe not, but you have to admit he's pretty distinctive-looking. There's no mistaking him for anyone else. So when I couldn't see you or Anna anywhere, I thought maybe Conan broke out of your place and was running loose. I was trying to grab hold of his collar so I could take him back to Brambleberry House when suddenly, who should show up but this extremely sexy guy who looked familiar in an odd sort of way?"

Sage didn't even want to think about just how extremely sexy *she* found Eben Spencer.

"He whistled to Conan and the two of them just kept running down the beach."

"That *is* strange," Sage murmured.

"I couldn't help but wonder what on earth our newest little camper's father was doing running with your dog at six in the morning. That *was* Chloe Spencer's hottie of a dad, wasn't it?"

Sage could feel warmth soak her cheeks. She could

only be grateful the coloring she inherited from the Italian side of her family hid her blushing.

"It was. Conan and I bumped into Eben this morning on our daily jog and he, uh, graciously offered to exercise Conan for me."

Lindsey raised an eyebrow—the one with the diamond stud in it. "You sure that's all there is to the story? I'm sensing more. Come on, give me all the juice."

She would *not* allow anything resembling a guilty expression to cross her features, she vowed. They shared one kiss, that's all, and she was absolutely not going to share that information with anyone else—especially not Lindsey, who had a vivid imagination and would be spinning this whole thing way out of control.

"What juice?" she said. "You think I spent the night ripping up the sheets with Eben Spencer while his daughter slept in the next room, then I kicked him out of bed so he could go take my dog for a run?"

Lindsey laughed. "Okay. Stupid hypothesis. I have a feeling if a woman had a man like that in bed, she wouldn't kick him out if the house was on fire, forget about making him walk her dog."

"He's here to buy The Sea Urchin and will only be in town for a few days. Not even long enough for a summer fling, if I were into that kind of thing. Which I most assuredly am not. It happened just as I told you. I was jogging past his house and he was outside and offered to take Conan for his jog. Since you know I'm not excessively fond of that particular activity myself, I decided I would be stupid to refuse."

"Too bad." Lindsey grinned. "I like my version better. For a man like that, I might reconsider my strict hands-off policy toward tourists."

"He's too old for you."

"Mr. Delarosa in his Speedo is too old. Eben Spencer? Not even close."

To her relief, Sage was spared having to continue the conversation by the arrival of the first campers.

She was showing the children how to identify the different tracks of birds in the sand—and doing her level best *not* to pay more than her usual attention to the front door—when it opened suddenly and a little dark-haired sprite rushed through and headed straight for her.

"Hi Sage! My dad says he went running with Conan this morning while I was still sleeping."

Her skin suddenly itchy and tight, she drew in a breath and lifted her gaze to find Eben standing a short distance away watching her out those glittering green eyes.

She couldn't read anything at all in his expression—regret, renewed heat, even mild interest.

Fine. She could pretend nothing happened, too. "True enough," she answered Chloe.

"Why didn't anybody wake me up?" she pouted. "I would have gone jogging, too!"

"Conan has pretty long legs, honey. It's hard for me to keep up with him sometimes."

"I'm a slow runner," Chloe said glumly, then her face lit up. "I could ride a bike, though. I do that sometimes back home. I ride my bike and my dad has to run to catch up with me."

Sage couldn't help giving Eben a quick look, endeared despite herself at the image of Eben jogging while his daughter rode her bike alongside.

It seemed incongruous with everything else she had discerned about the man—but she supposed one brief kiss didn't automatically make her an expert.

"If I can find a bike, can I go with you next time?"

"I don't know if there will *be* a next time," she pointed out. "You're leaving in a few days."

That apparently was the wrong thing to say. Chloe's bottom lip jutted out and her green eyes looked as wounded as if Sage had just kicked her in the shins.

"I don't want to go. I like it here. I like you and I like your dog and I like finding sand dollars."

Sage gave her a little hug. "It's fun going on vacation and meeting new people, isn't it? When you came in, did you notice that Lindsey has some sea glass in a jar? Whoever guesses how many pieces are inside gets a prize."

Distracted for the moment, Chloe's truculence faded. "Really? What kind of prize?"

"A toy stuffed sea otter. It's really cool."

"I bet I can win it! I'm really good at guessing stuff." Chloe rushed away, leaving Eben and Sage alone.

She was intensely aware of him, the smell of expensive cologne that clung to his skin, his tailored blue shirt, the crisp folds in his silk power tie.

His business attire ought to be a major turn-off for her. It should have reminded her just how very far apart they were.

She had always thought she preferred someone like Will, who wasn't afraid to get his hands dirty. But she couldn't seem to control the wild impulse to loosen that tie a little, to spread her hands over the strong muscles beneath the expensive tailoring.

She cleared her throat and forced herself to meet his still-veiled gaze. "Chloe should have a great day today. We have lots of fun things planned for the children."

"Great. I know she's excited—more excited than she's been about anything in a long time."

"That's what we like to hear."

"Okay, then. I guess I'll see you later."

He turned away and headed out the door. Sage watched him for only a moment—but even that was too long and too revealing, apparently. When she turned back to her campers she found her assistant director watching her with a knowing look.

"You know, it's really too bad you're not the kind of woman who would consider a summer fling," Lindsey murmured as Eben closed the door behind him.

Wasn't it? Sage thought, but she quickly turned her attention to the children.

* * *

He was dead meat.

Roast him, fry him, stick him on a spit. Sage Benedetto was going to kill him.

With one eye on the digital clock on the dashboard, Eben accelerated to pass a slow-moving minivan towing a pop-up trailer. He was supposed to have been at the nature center to pick up Chloe twenty minutes ago and he was still an hour away from Cannon Beach.

Sage might have disliked him before—their disturbing, heated morning kiss notwithstanding—but her mild antipathy was going to move into the territory of loathing if he didn't reach her soon to explain.

He was beyond tardy, approaching catastrophically, negligently late.

He steered the Jag off the highway and dialed the center's number again, as he had done a half-dozen times since the moment he had emerged late from meeting with his team of Portland attorneys.

He'd gotten a busy signal for the last half-hour, but this time to his relief the phone rang four times before someone picked up. He recognized Sage's low, sexy voice the moment she said hello.

"Hello. Eben Spencer here," he said, feeling far more awkward and uncomfortable than he was accustomed to.

Somehow she seemed to bring out the worst in him and he didn't like it at all.

"I've, uh, got a slight problem."

"Oh?"

"I'm afraid I'm just leaving Portland. I had a meeting that ran long and, to be perfectly honest, I wasn't paying attention to the time. I'm hurrying as fast as I can, but I won't be there for another hour, even if the traffic cooperates. I'm very sorry."

He heard a slight pause on the line and could almost hear her thinking what a terrible father he was. Right now, he couldn't say he disagreed.

"No problem," she finally said. "I'll just take her to Brambleberry House with me. Conan will be over the moon to see her again."

"I can't ask you to do that."

"You didn't ask. I offered. And anyway, I certainly can't leave her here by herself. I could take her to your beach house but I wouldn't feel right about leaving her alone there either. I don't mind taking her home with me. Like I said, Conan will love the company."

"In that case, thank you." He had to struggle not to grovel with gratitude.

Until this week when he'd been forced by circumstance to bring Chloe along, he wasn't sure he had fully comprehended how much he relied on nannies to take care of details like making sure Chloe was picked up on time. It was all a hell of a lot harder on his own.

He always considered himself a pretty good employer but he was definitely going to make sure he paid the next nanny more.

"You live in the big yellow Victorian down the beach, right?"

"Right. It's got a wrought-iron fence and a sign above the porch that says Brambleberry House."

"I'll be there as soon as I can." He paused. "Thank you again. I owe you."

"No problem. You can pay me back by taking Conan for another run in the morning."

Her words conjured up that kiss again, Sage all sleepy and warm and desirable in his arms, and his stomach muscles tightened.

"That's not much of a punishment. I enjoyed it more than he did," he said, his voice suddenly rough. He had to hope his sudden hunger didn't carry through the phone line. "I'll be glad for the chance to do it again."

"Don't speak too quickly. The weather forecast calls for a big storm the rest of tonight and in the morning. You'll be soaked before you even make it out the front door. I, on the other hand, will be warm and dry and cozy in my bed."

He didn't even want to go there. "I still think I'll be getting the better end of the stick, but you've got a deal."

"We'll see you in a while, then. And Eben, you really don't have to rush. Chloe will be fine."

He severed the connection and sat for a moment in the car, surrounded by lush green foliage in every direction.

He shouldn't be filled with anticipation at seeing her again. He couldn't afford the distraction—and even if he could, he shouldn't want so much to be distracted by *her*.

What was the point, really? He wasn't interested in anything short-term. How could he even think about it, with his eight-year-old daughter around? And he certainly wasn't looking for any kind of longer commitment or if he were, it would never be with a wild, free-spirited woman like Sage.

With a sigh, he put the Jag into gear again and pulled back onto the highway. Best to just work as hard as he could to finalize the deal with the Wus so he could take Chloe back to San Francisco, back to his comfort zone where everything was safe and orderly and predictable.

The storm Sage had mentioned hit just as he reached the outskirts of town. The lights of Brambleberry House gleamed in the pale, watery twilight, a beacon of warm welcome against the vast, dark ocean just beyond it.

The house was a bit more than she described, a rambling Queen Anne Victorian with a wide front porch, elaborate gingerbread trim and a voluptuous tangle of gardens out front. Painted a cheery yellow with multi-colored pastel accents, it looked bright and homey, the kind of place that for some reason always made him picture bread baking and the sweet, embracing scents of home.

He blinked the random image away and hurried through the rain to ring the doorbell, grateful for the wide porch that kept him mostly dry.

Despite the sign above the porch, he thought for a moment he might have come to the wrong house when a stranger answered the door. She had dark hair, solemn eyes, and an air about her of efficient competence.

Her mouth lifted in an impersonal, slightly wary smile. "Yes?"

"Hello. I was certain I was in the right place but now I'm beginning to doubt myself. This is Brambleberry House, isn't it?"

"Yes." She still kept the door only slightly ajar— probably a smart self-defense move so she could slam it quickly shut if he should try anything threatening.

"I'm Eben Spencer. I believe Sage Benedetto is expecting me."

She seemed to relax a little and the door opened wider, letting out a bigger slice of light and warmth to fight back the rainy evening. "You must be Chloe's father."

He held out a hand and she took it. Again, he gathered the vague impression of competence, though he wasn't sure what about her spoke so solidly of it.

"I'm Anna Galvez. I live on this floor and Sage is upstairs, all the way at the top."

"Which means you probably get roped into answering the door for her more often than you'd like."

Her smile warmed. "I don't mind, usually, unless I'm in the middle of something. Sage has a separate doorbell to her apartment but it hasn't been working for awhile. We're working on it. Sage's apartment is all the way to the top of the staircase."

The wide, sweeping staircase was the center core of the magnificent house, he saw, rising straight up from the entry through two other floors. A shame the house had been split into apartments, he thought. It would have made a stunning bed and breakfast, though he supposed it could be converted back if someone had the money, time and energy.

"Thank you," he said to Anna. "Sorry to bother you."

"Not a problem."

He followed the curve of stairs, his hand on the mahogany rail that had been worn smooth over generations.

Outside the door at the top, he heard laughter, then a dog's loud barking. He picked up Chloe's voice, then Sage's. The sound of it, rich and full and sexy, strummed down his spine.

He knocked and the dog's barking increased. He heard Sage order the dog to be stay and be quiet. It seemed to work—when she opened the door, Conan was sitting perfectly still beside the door, though he was practically vibrating with impatience.

Sage had changed yet again—the third outfit he'd seen her in that day. Instead of her jogging clothes or the conservative navy knit shirt and khaki slacks she wore to work, she wore a flowery tunic-style blouse in some kind of sheer material over a pale pink tank top, dangly earrings and a pair of faded jeans.

She looked heart-stoppingly gorgeous, lush and appealing, and he couldn't seem to focus on anything but their kiss that morning.

He knew he didn't mistake the memory of it flaring in her dark eyes. Her mouth parted slightly and beneath the memory was a faint sheen of trepidation.

Did she think he was going to grab her right here in front of her dog and his daughter for a repeat performance?

"You made good time from Portland." In seconds, she shunted away the brief flicker of remembered heat from her gaze and became as coolly polite as her downstairs neighbor.

"I was afraid you'd be ready to string me up if I didn't hurry."

"I told you not to worry about it. Chloe's a joy."

He raised an eyebrow at that, not used to hearing such praise of his daughter. Before he could respond, Chloe rushed to him.

"Hi Daddy! I had a *super* day today. We learned about the different habitats in the ocean at camp and then when we came here, we went outside on the beach and played catch with Conan and then we made lasagna with zucchini and carrots! It's almost ready. Sage says I can stay and have some. Can I, Daddy?"

He glanced at Sage and saw her mouth tighten slightly. He was quite certain the invitation would never have been extended if she had expected him to be here before the meal was ready.

But how could he disappoint Chloe by telling her they needed to go, that they had already imposed on Sage enough for the day?

Sage must have sensed his indecision. She smiled brightly, though it didn't quite reach her eyes. "You're certainly both welcome to stay. There's plenty for everyone and Chloe did work hard to help me fix it. It's only fair she get to enjoy the fruits of her labor."

"Did we put fruit in there too?" Chloe asked, a baffled expression on her face. "I thought it was just vegetables."

"Well, remember, technically tomatoes are a fruit. So I guess that counts. Seriously, you're both welcome to stay."

Though he knew it was a mistake to spend more time with Sage, he couldn't figure out any way out without hurting Chloe.

"All right. Thank you."

He was quite certain *he* was the one with trepidation in his eyes now as he stepped into her apartment. Only after he crossed the threshold did Conan hurry to him for attention and Eben could swear the dog looked pleased.

Chapter Six

Sage had always considered her apartment to be a perfect size, roomy without being huge. The rooms were all comfortably laid out and she loved having an extra bedroom in case any friends from college came to stay. It had always seemed just right for her.

How was it that Eben Spencer seemed to fill up every available inch?

His presence was overwhelming. He wore the same pale blue dress shirt he'd had on that morning, though his tie was off and his sleeves were rolled up. Afternoon stubble shadowed his jawline, giving him a slightly disreputable look she guessed he would probably find appalling if he were aware of it.

He looked so damn gorgeous, it was infuriating.

She shouldn't even be noticing how he looked, not after she had spent all day sternly reminding herself they had nothing in common, no possible reason for this unwanted attraction that simmered between them.

He represented wealth and privilege and all the things she had turned her back on after a lifetime of struggling—and failing—to find her place there. He was no doubt just like her father, obsessed with making and keeping his money.

Good grief, the cost of his tailored shirt alone could probably feed a family of four for a month.

She didn't like him, she told herself. While her brain might be certain of that, the rest of her was having a tougher time listening to reason when she just wanted to curl against his strength and heat like Conan finding a sunbeam shooting through the window.

She sighed and pulled her lasagna out, attributing her flushed and tight skin to the heat pouring from the oven.

"Can I help with anything?" he asked, standing in the doorway.

Yeah. Go away.

She forced herself to stuff the thought back into the recesses of her mind. She was a strong, independent woman. Surely she was tough enough to endure an hour or so with the man.

"Everything's just about ready. Chloe and I were finishing things up in here when you arrived. Would the two of you mind setting the table?"

She regretted the question as soon as she asked it.

Eben Spencer probably had a legion of servants to do that sort of grunt work at his house. To her surprise, he didn't hesitate.

"No problem. Come on, Chloe."

Through the doorway beyond him, Sage saw Chloe get up from the floor where she had been playing with Conan. She and the dog both tromped into the kitchen, making Sage even more claustrophobic.

"You'll have to point me in the right direction for plates and silverware," Eben said.

"I'll grab them for you."

She pulled out her favorite square chargers—she'd bought them from a ceramics studio in Manzanita, attracted by their wild, abstract designs—and the contrasting plates she always used with them, then held them out for Eben to take.

Their hands connected when he reached for them and a spark jumped between them.

Sage flushed. "Sorry. It's the, uh, hardwood floors. Makes electricity jump in the air, especially when there are a lot of negative ions flying around from the storm."

She was babbling, she realized, and forced herself to clamp her lips shut. She didn't miss the long, considering look Eben gave her.

"Oh, is that what it's from?" he murmured.

Before she could formulate what would no doubt be a sharp retort, he grabbed the plates and carried them out of the kitchen. Only after he left did she release the breath she suddenly realized she was holding.

"Silverware is in the top drawer to the left of the dishwasher," she told Chloe. "Glasses are in the overhead cupboard."

She didn't have the luxury of a dining room in her apartment, but she had commandeered a corner of the good-sized living room for the table Will Garrett had made her.

The chairs were a mismatched jumble picked up here and there at thrift stores and yard sales, but she coordinated them with cushions in vivid colors to match the placemats and chargers.

She always thought the effect was charming but she imagined to someone of Eben Spencer's sophisticated tastes, her house probably reeked of a lousy attempt at garage-sale chic.

She didn't care, she told herself.

It was a waste of time even worrying about what he might think of her and her apartment. In a week, Eben and Chloe Spencer would just be a memory, simply two more in a long line of transitory visitors to her corner of the world.

The thought left her vaguely depressed so she pushed it away and pulled the salad she and Chloe had tossed earlier out of the refrigerator. After a few more moments of them working together, the meal was laid out on the table.

"Everything looks delicious," Eben said, taking the seat across from her.

"Sage is a vegetarian, Daddy," Chloe announced with fascinated eagerness.

"Is that right?"

"Not militant, I promise," she answered. "Steak lovers are usually still welcome at my table."

A corner of his mouth lifted. "Good thing. I do enjoy a good porterhouse, I'm sorry to say."

"You can enjoy it all you want somewhere else, but I'm afraid you won't find any steaks here tonight."

"I can be surprisingly adaptable." Again that half smile lifted his features, made him seem much less formidable. Her insides trembled but she stubbornly ignored them, serving the lasagna instead.

They were all quiet for a few moments as they dished breadsticks and salad.

Sage braced herself for a negative reaction to her favorite lasagna dish. She wasn't the greatest of cooks but after choosing a vegetarian lifestyle in college, she had worked hard to find dishes she found good, nutritious and filling.

But her tastes were likely far different than Eben's. He probably had at least one Cordon Bleu-trained personal chef to go along with the legion of servants she'd imagined for him.

To her relief and gratification, he closed his eyes in appreciation after the first taste. "Delicious. My compliments to the chefs."

Chloe giggled. "There weren't any chefs, Daddy. Just Sage and me."

"You two have outdone yourselves."

"It's super good, Sage," Chloe agreed. "I wasn't sure I'd like it but I can't even taste the carrots and stuff."

Sage smiled, charmed all over again by this little girl with the inquisitive mind and boundless energy.

"Thank you both. I'm glad you're enjoying it."

"Maybe you could give me the recipe and I could make it sometime at home, if the new nanny helps me," Chloe suggested. "I like to cook stuff sometimes, when I have a chance."

"I'll do that. Remind me before you leave and I'll make a copy of the recipe for you."

"Thank you very much," Chloe said, with a solemn formality that made Sage smile again. She shifted her gaze from the girl to her father and immediately wished she hadn't.

Eben watched her, an odd expression in those brilliant green eyes. It left her breathless and off balance. He quickly veiled it in that stiff, controlled way of his she was coming to despise.

"This is a beautiful house," he said into the sudden silence. "Have you lived here long?"

"Five years or so—I moved in a few weeks after I came to Cannon Beach."

"You're not from here? I wondered. You have a slight northeast accent every once in a while, barely noticeable."

Her mouth tightened as if she could clamp down all trace of the past she didn't like remembering. "Boston," she finally said.

"That's what I would have guessed. So what brought you to Oregon?"

"When I graduated from Berkeley, I took an internship at the nature center. I spent the first few weeks in town renting a terrible studio apartment a few blocks from here. It was all I could afford on an intern's salary, which was nothing."

"You worked for free?" Chloe asked and Sage had to smile a little at the shock in her voice.

"I was fresh out of college and ready to see the world, try anything. But I did hate living in that terrible apartment."

"How did you end up here?" Eben asked. He sounded genuinely interested, she realized, feeling ashamed of herself for being so surprised by it.

"One day at the grocery store I helped a local woman with her bags and she invited me home for dinner." Her heart spasmed a little and she suddenly missed Abigail desperately.

She managed a smile, though she suspected it didn't look very genuine. "I've been here every since."

Eben was silent for a long moment. By the time he spoke, Sage had regained her composure.

"How many apartments are in this place?"

"Three. One on each floor, but the middle floor is empty right now."

"Your neighbor on the first floor let me in."

"Right. Anna."

Conan barked a little from under the table when she

said Anna's name and Sage covered her annoyance by taking a sip of the wine she had set out for her and Eben.

Eben and Anna Galvez would be perfect for each other. The hotel tycoon and the sharp, focused businesswoman. They were both type A personalities, both probably had lifetime subscriptions to *The Wall Street Journal*, both probably knew exactly the difference between the Dow Jones and the NASDAQ—and how much of their respective portfolios were tied up in each, down to the penny.

Sage could barely manage to balance her checkbook most months and still carried a balance on her credit card from paying a down-on-his-luck friend's rent a few months earlier.

Yeah, Eben and Anna would make a good pair. So why did the idea of the two of them together leave her feeling vaguely unsettled?

"You said the second floor is empty?"

"Yes. We're still trying to figure out what we want to do, whether we want to fix it up and rent it out or leave things as is. Too many decisions to make all at once."

"I didn't understand that you owned the place. I thought you were renting."

She made a face. "I own it as of a month ago. Well, sort of."

"How do you sort of own something?"

"Anna and I co-inherited the place and everything in it, including Conan."

He looked intrigued and she didn't like feeling her

life was one interesting puzzle for him to solve. "So the dog came with the house?" he asked.

"Something like that."

"So are you and Anna related in some way?"

"Nope." She sipped at her wine. "It's a long story."

She didn't want to talk about Abigail so she deliberately changed the subject.

"I understand from Chloe you're in town to buy The Sea Urchin from Stanley and Jade Wu."

Frustration flickered in his green eyes. "That's the plan, anyway."

"When do you expect to close the sale?"

"Good question. There have been a few…complications."

"Oh?"

"Everything was supposed to be done by now but I'm afraid the Wus are having second thoughts. I'm still working hard to convince them."

"My daddy has a lot of other hotels," Chloe piped up, "but he really, really wants The Sea Urchin."

Of course. No doubt it was all about the game to him, the acquisition of more and more. Just like her own father, who had virtually abandoned his child to the care of others, simply to please his narcissistic, self-absorbed socialite of a second wife.

"And I imagine whatever you want, you get, isn't that right?"

She meant to keep her voice cool and uninterested,

but she was fairly sure some of her bitterness dripped
into her words.

He studied her for a long moment, long enough that
she felt herself flush at her rudeness. He didn't deserve
to bear the brunt of an old, tired hurt that had nothing
to do with him.

"Not always," he murmured.

"Can I have another breadstick?" Chloe asked into
the sudden awkward silence.

Her father turned his attention to her. "How many
have you had? Four, isn't it?"

"They're so good, though!"

Sage had enough experience with both eight-year-
olds and dogs to know exactly where the extra bread-
sticks were going—under the table, where Conan
lurked, waiting patiently for anything tossed his way.

She handed Chloe another breadstick with a conspiratorial smile. "This is the last one, so you'd better
make it last."

"I'm going to have to roll you down the stairs, I'm
afraid."

Chloe snickered at her father. "Conan could help you
carry me down. He's way strong."

"Stronger than me, probably, especially with all those
breadsticks in his system."

Chloe jerked her hand above the table surface with
a guilty look, but her father didn't reprimand her, he
only smiled.

Sage gazed at his light expression with frustration.

Drat the man. Just when she thought she had him pegged, he had to act in a way that didn't match her perception.

It was becoming terribly difficult to hang on to her dislike of him. Though her first impression of him had been of a self-absorbed businessman with little time for his child, she was finding it more difficult to reconcile that with a man who could tease his daughter into the giggles.

She had always made a practice of looking for the good in people. Even during the worst of her childhood she had tried to find her stepmother's redeeming qualities. So why was she so determined to only see negatives when she looked at Eben Spencer?

Maybe she was afraid to notice his good points. If she could still be so attracted to him when she was only focusing on the things she disliked, how much more vulnerable would she be if she allowed herself to see the good in him?

The thought didn't sit well at all.

What was her story? Eben wondered as Sage dished out a simple but delicious dessert of vanilla ice cream and fresh strawberries. She was warm and approachable one moment, stiff and cool the next. She kissed like a dream then turned distant and polite.

Her house was like her—eclectic, colorful, with a bit of an eccentric bent. One whole display case in the corner was filled with gnarled pieces of driftwood interspersed with various shells and canning jars filled with polished glass. Nothing in the house looked extravagant or costly, but it all seemed to work together to make a charming, cozy nest.

He was intensely curious about how she came to own the house after five years of renting it, but she obviously hadn't want to talk about it so he had let her turn the conversation in other directions. He wondered if that had something to do with the pain that sometimes flickered in her gaze.

"I *love* strawberries," Chloe announced. "They're my very favorite thing to have on ice cream."

"You need to try some of the Oregon berries sometime," Sage said with a smile.

She maintained none of her stiff reserve with Chloe. She was genuinely warm all the time and he found it entrancing.

"And before you leave, remind me to give you some of the wild raspberry jam I made last summer," she went on.

"You made jam all by yourself?"

"It's not hard. The toughest thing is not eating the berries the minute you pick them so you've got enough left to use for the jam."

Before Chloe could ask the million question Eben could see forming in her eyes, Sage's dog slithered out from under the table and began to bark insistently.

"Uh-oh. That's his ignore-me-at-your-peril bark," Sage said quickly, setting her unfinished dessert down on the table. "I had better let him out."

"I'll do it!" Chloe exclaimed. Her features—so much like her mother's—were animated and excited.

She had been remarkably well-behaved through dinner—no tantrums, no power struggles. It was a refreshing change, he thought. Sage Benedetto had a remarkably positive effect on her. He wasn't sure what she did differently, but Chloe responded to her in a way his daughter hadn't to anyone else in a long time.

"Thanks, Chloe," Sage said. "Just make sure the gate is closed around the yard so he can't take off. He's usually pretty good about staying on his own territory, but all bets are off if he catches sight of a cat."

Chloe paused at the door. "Can I ask Miss Galvez if I can look at the dolls while I'm downstairs?"

Sage shifted her gaze to meet Eben's. "You'll have to ask your father that."

"Someone will have to clue me in. What dolls?"

"The woman who left the house to me and to Anna Galvez had a huge doll collection. It takes up an entire room in Anna's apartment now. I promised Chloe we could take a look at them before dinner, but time slipped away from us and then you arrived."

"Can I see it, Daddy?"

"If Miss Galvez doesn't mind showing you, I can't see any reason why not."

"Yay!" Chloe raced out the door, though Conan shot ahead of her and Eben could hear his paws click furiously down the stairs.

The moment they left, Eben realized he was alone with Sage—not a comfortable situation given the tension still simmering between them. She was obviously suddenly cognizant of that fact as well. She jerked to her feet and started clearing away their dinner dishes.

He finished the last of his dessert and rose to help her. "Thank you again for dinner. I can't remember a meal I've enjoyed more."

It was true, he realized with surprise. Chloe was usually in bed when he returned home from work, but on the rare occasions he dined with her, he typically found himself bracing for her frequent emotional outbursts.

It had been wonderful to enjoy his daughter's company under Sage's moderating influence.

Sage didn't look convinced by his words. "It was only vegetarian lasagna. Probably nothing at all like you're used to. You don't have to patronize me."

Her words surprised a laugh from him. "I don't think I could patronize you, even if I tried. I doubt anyone can. I mean it. I enjoyed the meal—and the company—immensely."

She studied him for a moment then nodded. "So did I."

"You sound surprised. It's not very flattering, I must admit."

"I am surprised, I suppose. I don't entertain a great deal. When I do, it's usually friends in my own circle."

"I appreciate you making an exception in our case."

He was intensely aware of her, of the way her dangly earrings caught the lamplight, the smell of her, feminine and enticing, her mobile expressions. He wanted to kiss her again, with a fierce ache, though he knew it was impossible, not to mention extremely unwise.

He didn't want to destroy this fragile peace—especially when his intentions could never be anything other than a quick fling, something he guessed wasn't typical for her, either.

In an effort to cool his growing awareness, he searched his mind for a change of topic as he followed her into the small kitchen with his hands full of dishes.

"Tell me the truth, now that Chloe is gone for a moment. How was she today?"

Surprise widened her eyes at the question. "Fine. She's a little energetic, but no worse than any of the other eight-year-olds at the camp. Better than some. She's very sweet."

She studied him and he was certain some of his relief must have shown on his features.

"You look like you expected a different answer."

He sighed and put the dishes down on the countertop next to the sink. "I love my daughter, but I have to admit that *sweet* is not an adjective many people use to describe her these days."

"That surprises me. She seems to me a typical kid, just like the others in the class."

"I think you have an extraordinary rapport with her.'"

"I'm not sure why that would be."

"I'm not, either. Chloe is…challenging. She's bright and creative and funny most of the time, but she has these mood swings. Her mother's death two years ago affected her strongly. She and Brooke were very close. Her mother doted on her—maybe too much."

"I don't think you can ever love a child too much."

There was that stiffness in her voice again. "I don't, either. Please don't misunderstand. I only meant that losing her mother was a fierce and painful blow to Chloe. As a parent, I'm afraid I'm a poor substitute for my wife."

Her gaze flashed to his and he regretted exposing so much truth about himself.

"I tried to give her some leeway for her grief for several months but I'm afraid I let her get away with too many things and now that's her expectation all the time. In the last year and a half she's been through four schools and a half-dozen nannies. She's moody and unpredictable. Defiant one moment, deceptively docile the next."

Without really thinking about it, he started to load the dishes in the dishwasher. "The other morning was a perfect example," he continued. "She could have been seriously hurt sneaking out so early. I wouldn't do as she demanded the night before and stay out late hunting up seashells with her, so she countermanded me by sneaking out on her own."

She opened her mouth slightly then closed it again.

"What were you going to say?" he pressed.

"Nothing. Never mind." She turned away to run water in the sink for the soiled dishes.

Eben leaned against the counter next to her, enjoying her graceful movements.

"You probably would have been right out there with her in the middle of the night with a flashlight and a bucket looking for sand dollars, wouldn't you?"

She gave him a sidelong look, then smiled. "Probably."

"I let her get away with too much right after Brooke died and I need to set some boundaries now. Children needs rules and structure."

"Is that the kind of childhood you had? Regimented, toe-the-line. Military school, right?"

He laughed, though he heard the harsh note in it and wondered if she did as well. "Not quite. I would have given my entire baseball card collection for a little structure and discipline. My parents were of the if-it-feels-good-just-do-it school of thought. It destroyed them both and they nearly took me and my sister along with them. I can't do that to Chloe."

Her hands paused in the sink and her eyes widened with sympathy. He shifted, uncomfortable. Where the hell had that come from? He didn't share these pieces of his life with anyone. He wasn't sure he'd ever even articulated that to Brooke. If he had, maybe she wouldn't have expected so many things from him he wasn't at all sure he had been capable of offering.

He certainly had no business sharing them with Sage. She was quiet for a long moment, watching him out of intense brown eyes. The only sound was the rain clicking against the window and the soft sound of their mingled breathing.

"I'm sorry," she finally murmured.

He shrugged. "It was a long time ago. I just don't want to make the same mistakes with Chloe."

"But you can go too far in the other direction, can't you?"

"I'm doing my best. That's all I can do."

He didn't want to talk about this anymore. With her so close, he was having a tough time hanging on to any coherent thought anyway. All he could think about was kissing her again.

But he couldn't.

The thought had no sooner entered his head than he could swear he felt a soft hand in the small of his back from out of nowhere pushing him toward her.

She gave him a quick startled look then her gaze seemed to fasten on his mouth.

What other choice did he have but to kiss her?

Chapter Seven

She sighed as if she'd been waiting for his kiss and she tasted heady and sweet from the wine and the strawberries.

Having her in his arms felt *right*, in a way he couldn't explain. On an intellectual level, it made absolutely no sense and every voice in his head was clamoring to tell him why kissing her again was a colossal mistake.

He shut them all out and focused only on the silky smoothness of her hair, her soft curves against him.

Her hands were warm, wet from the dishwater. He could feel the palm prints she left against his shirt, a temporary brand.

He had been thinking of their earlier kiss all day. As

he drove to Portland and back, as he listened to his attorneys ramble on and on. Like the low murmur of the sea outside, she had been a constant presence in his mind. Their kiss that morning had been heated and intense, more so because it had been so unexpected.

This, though, was different. Eben closed his eyes at the astonishing gentleness of it, the quiet peace that seemed to swirl around them, wrapping them together with silken threads.

He still wanted her fiercely and the hunger thrumming inside him urged him to deepen the kiss but he kept it slow and easy, reluctant to destroy the fragile beauty of the moment.

"All day long, I've been telling myself a thousand reasons why I shouldn't do that again," he murmured after a long, drugging moment.

He could see a pulse flutter in her throat, feel her chest rise and fall with her accelerated breathing. She dropped her hands from his shirt, but not before he was certain he felt their slight tremble.

"I can probably give you a couple thousand more why I shouldn't have let you."

"Yet here we are."

She sighed and he heard turmoil and regret in the sound. "Right. Here we are."

She stepped away from him and immersed her hands in the dishwater, a slight brush of color on her cheeks as she started scrubbing a pan with fierce concentration.

He sighed, compelled to honesty. "I'm not looking

for anything. You need to know that. This just sort of…
happened."

The temperature in the room suddenly seemed to dip
a dozen degrees and he could swear the rain lashed the
windows with much more force than before.

When she spoke, her voice was as cool as the rain.
"That makes two of us, then."

"Right."

He was digging himself in deeper but he had to attempt
an explanation. "We just have this…thing between us. I
have to tell you, I don't quite understand it."

"Don't you?" Her voice was positively icy now and
he realized how his words could be construed.

He sighed again, hating this awkward discomfort.
"You're a beautiful woman, Sage. You have to know
that. Any man would be crazy not to find you attractive.
But I swear, until this morning I have never in my life
kissed a woman I haven't at least taken on two or three
dates. I've never known anything like this. You just do
something to me. I can't explain it. To be honest, I'm
not sure I like it."

The ice in her eyes had thawed a little, he saw, though
he wasn't sure he was thrilled with the shadow of amuse-
ment that replaced it.

"I'm sure you don't."

"I haven't dated in a decade," he confessed. "My wife
and I were married for seven years and Brooke has been
gone for two years now. I'm afraid I'm out of practice
at this whole man–woman thing."

She sent him a sidelong look he couldn't read. "I wouldn't exactly say that."

Oddly, he could swear he heard a ripple of low laughter coming from the other room. He shifted his gaze to the doorway into her living room and saw Sage do the same, almost as if she could hear it, too.

No one was there, he could tell in an instant, but his attention was suddenly caught by a picture he hadn't noticed before hanging on the wall of the kitchen.

He stared at the image of two women on what looked like a sea cliff, their cheeks pressed together as they embraced, deep affection in their eyes.

One was Sage, a lighthearted joy in her expression he hadn't seen before. But his shock of recognition was for the other person, the one with the wrinkled features and mischievous eyes.... He moved closer for a better look.

"I know this woman!"

Sage blinked a little at his abrupt change of topic. "Abigail? You know Abigail?"

"Yes! Abigail, that's her name!"

"Abigail Dandridge. She's the one who left me this house. She was my best friend in the world."

"I never knew her last name. She's dead, then." An obvious statement, but he couldn't for the world think of what else to say.

She nodded, her eyes suddenly dark with emotion. "It's been almost five weeks now. Her heart just stopped in her sleep one night. No warning signs at all. I know she would have wanted to go that way, but...I didn't have a chance to say goodbye—you know?—and everything feels so *unfinished*. I still feel her here, in the house. At random moments I think I smell her favorite scent or feel the touch of her hand in my hair. It's a cliché, but I still keep thinking I'll hear her voice any minute now, calling me down the stairs to share some gossip over tea."

He suddenly understood the sorrow he glimpsed every once in a while in Sage's eyes. He wanted to comfort her but couldn't find the words, not through his own shock and sadness.

She looked at him with puzzlement in her eyes. "I'm sorry. How did you say you knew her?"

"I suppose I can't really say I knew her. I met her only briefly but the encounter was...unforgettable."

She smiled, a little tremulously. "Abigail often had that effect on people."

"I should have figured it out. You know, I thought Conan looked familiar but I didn't put the pieces together until right this moment. I can't believe she's gone."

"You met her then? She didn't say anything about it."

"It probably wasn't as significant a meeting for her as it was for me. I came to town scouting locations for a new property. I was jogging early one morning and I saw her and I guess it was Conan. I don't know why I stopped to talk to her—maybe I stopped to tie my shoe or something—but we struck up a conversation. It was the oddest thing. After we talked for awhile, she insisted on taking me to breakfast at The Sea Urchin—and I went, which isn't at all like me."

What also hadn't been like him was the way the woman's warm, kind eyes had led him to telling her far more about himself than he did with most people.

By the time they'd finished their divine breakfast of old-fashioned French toast with mountains of fresh whipped cream and bacon so crisp it melted in his mouth, Abigail knew about Chloe, about Brooke's death, even about those last years of their troubled marriage.

"Abigail was always doing things like that, grabbing a stranger to take out for a meal," Sage said into his sudden silence. "She loved to meet new people. She used to say she knew everything there was to know about the locals and she got damn sick and tired of hearing the same boring old stories a hundred times."

"She was wonderful. Sharp. Funny. Kind. After breakfast at The Sea Urchin, she suggested I talk to Stanley and Jade Wu about buying it. You know, the whole thing was her idea. She told me they were thinking about retiring, but I have to say, until I approached them with an offer, I don't think it had even occurred to them to sell the place."

"I told you Abigail knew everything about the locals, sometimes things they didn't even know themselves."

Abigail had certainly been able to see deep into Sage's own mind. From the moment Sage arrived in Cannon Beach, Abigail had seemed to know instinctively how much Sage longed for a family and home of her own.

The remarkable thing had been her way of finding the best in everyone she met and helping them see it as well.

Why on earth would Abigail have picked Eben Spencer to be one of her pet projects? Sage couldn't for the life of her figure it out. And she had steered him toward buying The Sea Urchin? It didn't make sense. Abigail would never have suggested he buy the place if she didn't trust him to take care of it.

Maybe Sage needed to reconsider her perceptions of the man. If Abigail had approved of him to that extent, perhaps she saw deeper into him than Sage could.

"That morning at breakfast with Abigail felt like an omen. I have to admit, from the moment we stepped into the place, I set my heart on purchasing The Sea Urchin and I'm afraid I haven't been able to even entertain the idea of any other property for Spencer Hotels' next project. I'm only sorry I didn't have the chance to meet up with her again."

What weird twist of fate had led her to Chloe on the beach that morning, to someone peripherally connected to Abigail? Or *had* it been a coincidence? She shivered a little, remembering how Conan had greeted Chloe like an old friend, as if he had been expecting her.

"Everything okay?" Eben asked.

He would probably mock any woo-woo speculation on her part. She had a feeling Eben was a prosaic man not given to superstition.

"Fine. Just thinking how odd it was that you're here now, in Abigail's house."

"*Your* house, now."

"In my mind, it will always belong to her. She loved every inch of this place."

Before he could answer, they heard footsteps bounding up the stairs. A moment later, Chloe and Conan burst into the apartment, with Anna Galvez in tow.

"Daddy, Daddy, guess what?"

"What, sweetheart?"

"There's a whole room of dolls downstairs. It's huge. I've never *seen* so many dolls. Miss Galvez says if it's okay with you, I can pick one out and keep it. May I, Daddy? Oh please, may I?"

"Chloe—" He shifted, obviously uncomfortable with the idea.

Sage sent a swift look to Anna, surprised she would make such an offer. She wouldn't have expected such a generous gesture from Anna, especially after their conversation the day before about keeping the collection intact.

But somehow it seemed exactly the right thing to do, precisely what Abigail would have wanted, for them to give this sweet daughter of the man Abigail had known one of her beloved dolls.

"Several of the dolls have resin faces and aren't breakable. They're completely safe for her," Anna said somewhat stiffly.

Eben looked at Sage with a question in his eyes. She nodded. "Abigail would have wanted her things to be loved," she said. "She adored showing them off to children."

She got the impression it wasn't an easy thing for Eben to accept anything from anyone. He was a hard, self-contained man, though it appeared he had a soft spot for his daughter, something she wouldn't have expected just a few days before.

"All right," he finally said. "If you're certain you don't mind."

Chloe squealed with excitement. "You have to help me choose one. Both of you."

She grabbed Sage with one hand then Eben with the other and started tugging them both toward the stairs. Conan barked once and Sage could swear he was grinning again.

She didn't know which she found more disturbing, her dog's pleased expression or Anna's speculative one.

For the next ten minutes, she, Anna and Eben helped Chloe peruse Abigail's vast collection, doing their best to point her toward the sturdier, more age-appropriate dolls.

Sage had never been one to play with girlie things, but even she had to admit how much she enjoyed walking into the doll room. She couldn't help feeling close to Abigail here, amid the collection that had been such a part of her friend.

Abigail never married and had no children of her own. She had a great-nephew somewhere, but he hadn't even bothered coming to his great-aunt's funeral. In many ways, the dolls were Abigail's family, the inanimate counterpoints to the living, breathing strays she collected.

Sage loved seeing them, remembering the joy

Abigail had found every time she added a new doll to her collection.

She especially loved the dolls Abigail had made herself over the decades, with painted faces and elaborate hand-sewn clothes. Victorian dolls with flounced dresses and parasols, teenyboppers with ponytails and poodle skirts, dolls with bobbed hair and flapper dresses.

There was no real rhyme or reason to the collection—no common theme that Sage had ever been able to discern—but each was charming in its own way.

"I can't decide. There are too many."

A spasm of irritation crossed Eben's features at Chloe's whiny tone. Sage could tell the girl was tired after their big day on the shore then coming back to Brambleberry House afterward. She hoped Eben was perceptive enough to pick up on that as well.

To her relief, after only a moment his frustration slid away, replaced by patience. He pulled his daughter close and kissed her on the top of her dark curls and Sage could swear she felt her heart tumble in her chest.

"Pick out your favorite three and maybe we can help you make your final choice," he suggested, a new gentleness in his voice.

That seemed a less daunting task to his daughter. With renewed enthusiasm she studied the shelves of dolls, pulling one out here and there, returning another, choosing with care until she had three lined up in the middle of the floor.

They were an oddly disparate trio: a little girl with

pigtails holding a teddy bear, a curvy woman in a grass Hawaiian skirt and lei, then an elegant woman with blond hair and a white dress.

Chloe studied them for a moment, then reached for the one in white. "You don't have to help me pick. This is the one I want. She looks just like an angel."

The doll was simple but lovely. "Good choice," Sage said, admiring the doll when Chloe held her out.

"Her name is Brooke."

"Of course it is," Eben murmured.

Sage glanced at him and was surprised to see a pained look in his eyes as he studied the doll. Only then did she remember his wife's name had been Brooke.

For the first time, Sage picked up the resemblance in the doll's features to Chloe's. Only their hair color was different.

Chloe must have picked the doll because it looked like her mother. Oh, poor little pumpkin. Sage wanted to gather her up and hold her tight until she didn't hurt anymore.

So much pain in the world.

"I'm going to put her on my bureau at home," Chloe announced. "That way I can see her every morning."

"Good plan," Anna said. Her eyes met Sage's and Sage could see her own supposition mirrored there.

"Okay, kiddo," Eben interjected, the shadows still in his gaze, "you need to say thanks to Sage and Ms. Galvez for the doll, then we should head home. You've had a big day and need to get some rest so you'll be a good little camper in the morning."

"Thank you very much for the doll. I will love her forever," the girl said solemnly to them, then turned back to her father. "I'm not tired at all, though. I would like to stay longer."

Eben smiled, Sage could see the lines around the corners of his mouth that only served to make him look more ruggedly handsome.

"*You* might not be tired, but I certainly am and I imagine Sage and Ms. Galvez are as well. Come on, let's take your new friend home."

Chloe paused, then ran to Anna and threw her arms around her waist. "I mean it. Thank you for the doll. I'll take super good care of her, I promise."

Anna looked discomfited by the girl's hug, but there was a softness in her eyes Sage hadn't seen before. "I'm glad to hear that. Bring her back anytime to see the rest of her friends."

Chloe giggled, then turned to Sage and embraced her as well. That tumble in her heart before was nothing compared to the hard, swift fall she felt as she fell head over heels for this sweet, motherless little girl.

"Thank you for letting me help you make vegetable lasagna and play with Conan and see where you live. I think Brambleberry House is the most beautiful house in the world."

Sage hugged her back. "You're very welcome. I'll see you in the morning, okay? Don't forget your raincoat. We're in for some nice Oregon sunshine. That means rain, by the way."

Chloe giggled, then slipped her hand in her father's.

Though Anna and Conan stayed in her apartment, Sage followed them outside. The rain had nearly stopped and only a light drizzle fell.

On the porch, she stopped, feeling as awkward as if they'd been on a date. That stunning, gentle kiss in her apartment seemed to shimmer through her mind and she couldn't seem to think of anything but his warm mouth and his strong, hard arms around her.

Though Chloe ran ahead and climbed into the back seat of the Jag, Eben paused and met her gaze, the recessed porch lights reflecting in his eyes. He grabbed her hand, his fingers enfolded around hers. "Thank you again for taking Chloe later than you planned, and for dinner and everything."

"You're very welcome. She was no trouble."

"Only because you're amazing with her."

Sage shook her head, slipping her hand from his, needing the safety of physical distance from him even as her emotions seemed to tug her ever nearer. "I find her a joy. I told you that."

"I'll be ready in the morning to run with Conan."

"I promise, I won't hold you to that. I was joking."

"I'm looking forward to it. This morning was wonderful and I'd love a repeat. The, uh, run I meant."

She was certain if the light had been brighter she would have seen faint color on his features. Somehow his discomfort over their unexpected kiss charmed her beyond measure.

She didn't need to spend more time with him or with Chloe. Both of them were already sneaking their way into her heart. More time would only make their departure that much more difficult. She already dreaded thinking about when they left Cannon Beach.

"Don't count on it," she answered. "If I'm lucky, my furry alarm clock will sleep in tomorrow."

"I'll be waiting if he doesn't."

Without another word, he turned and hurried down the steps into the drizzle.

Chapter Eight

Long after the car drove away, headlights reflecting on the wet streets, Sage stood on the porch of Brambleberry House, hugging her arms to her against the evening chill and worrying.

She had to find it in her heart to push them both away. That was the only solution. Her emotions were too battered right now, raw and aching from Abigail's death.

She wasn't strong enough to sustain another devastating loss. That's what it would be, she feared, if she let them inside any farther. She was afraid she would find it entirely too easy to fall for both of them. Already she was halfway to being in love with Chloe, with her sweet eyes and her quirky sense of humor and her desperate eagerness to please.

She sighed as an owl called somewhere in the distance, then Sage opened the door into the house.

She expected Anna to be cloistered in Abigail's apartment by the time she returned. Instead, she found her waiting in the foyer, one hand absently rubbing Conan's head. She looked softer, somehow, more approachable—perhaps because she'd changed out of her work clothes while Sage, Eben and Chloe had been upstairs having dinner.

She should have invited Anna to join them, she thought, ashamed of herself for not thinking of it.

"Thank you for the whole doll thing," she said. "It seemed to be a big hit with Chloe."

"I probably should have talked to you first about giving her one before I suggested it to her. I know what you said the other day about the collection staying together. Technically, they belong to both of us and they're not really mine to give away."

Would she ever escape the complexities of that blasted will? "Despite what you might think, I honestly don't want to hoard all of Abigail's things forever, to freeze everything in the house just as it is and never alter so much as a nail hole."

"I know you don't," Anna said stiffly. "I'm sorry if I gave you the impression I thought otherwise."

Sage sighed. "I'm sorry to be short with you. This is all so awkward, isn't it?"

Anna was quiet for a moment. "I know you loved Abigail deeply and she felt the same way about you.

There was an unbreakable bond between the two of you. Everyone could see it. I understand how painful her death is for you. Believe me, I understand. Maybe you loved her longer but...I loved her, too. I miss her."

Guilt lodged in her throat at her weeks of coldness toward Anna, at her ridiculous resentment—as if it were Anna's fault they found themselves in this tangled arrangement.

She had never felt so small and petty.

Abigail would have been furious with her, would have given her a stern look out of those blue eyes and told her to put on her big girl panties and just deal.

"Would you...like to come in?" Anna asked at Sage's continued silence. "I was about to have some tea and you're welcome to share it. You don't have to, of course."

She was exhausted suddenly, emotionally and physically. Her day had been tumultuous from that first kiss in Eben's beach house and she wanted nothing more than to climb into her bed and yank the quilt over her head and shut out the world.

But how could she rebuff such a clearcut overture of friendship?

"Sure. Okay."

Anna looked surprised, then thrilled, which only added to Sage's guilt level. The other woman led the way into her apartment, toward the little kitchen that still looked as it had the day Abigail died. Her gaze landed on the calendar still turned back to April and Abigail's handwritten little notes in the date squares.

Conan, shots, 10:30.
Lunch with the girls.
Will's birthday.

It was a snapshot of her life, busy and fulfilling. Why hadn't Anna taken it down? Sage would have thought that to be one of the first things an efficient, orderly woman like Anna would make an effort to do when she moved her own things in.

Did she find some kind of comfort from this small reminder of Abigail and her life? Sage resolved to try harder to forge a connection with Anna.

"What kind of tea would you like? I think there's every kind imaginable here."

Chai was her favorite but she wasn't sure she could drink it here in this kitchen out of Abigail's favorite teacups, not with her emotions so close to the surface.

"It's late. I don't need more caffeine with my head already buzzing. I'd better go for chamomile."

Anna smiled and found teabags in the cupboard, then pulled a burbling kettle off the stove and poured it over the bags.

Sage watched for a moment, awkward at the silence. "Thank you again for the doll thing," she said. "It was a great idea. Chloe was thrilled."

"She picked an angel doll and named her Brooke. Am I crazy or was there some deeper significance to that?"

"It was her mother's name."

Anna pursed her lips in distress. "That's what I thought. Poor little thing."

Anna studied her for a moment as if she wasn't sure whether to ask the questions Sage could see forming in her eyes. "You do know that's Eben Spencer, the CEO of Spencer Hotels, right?" she finally said.

"I hope so. If not, he's doing a fairly credible job of masquerading as the man."

"And do you realize he's brilliant? I read about him in *Fortune* a few months ago. The man has single-handedly rescued a small, floundering hotel company and turned it into a major player in the hospitality industry with small luxury properties around the globe."

"Yippee for him."

And she had fed him vegetarian lasagna and bread-sticks at her dining table with the mismatched chairs. She wanted a do-over on the whole evening.

No, she corrected herself. She wouldn't allow him to make her feel ashamed of her life or what she had worked hard to build for herself. After severing the last fragile ties with her father, she had started with nothing and had built a rich, fulfilling life here.

"While we were looking at the dolls, Chloe told me he's looking to buy The Sea Urchin."

"That's what I understand."

"It's a perfect property for Spencer Hotels. It will be interesting to see what he can do with the place."

"I like The Sea Urchin exactly the way it is," she muttered.

"So do I," Anna assured her. "But Spencer Hotels has

a reputation for taking great properties and making them even better. It will be interesting to watch."

"If Stanley and Jade ultimately decide to sell. I don't believe Eben has convinced them yet."

"If what I've heard about him is halfway true, he will." She paused and gave Sage a careful look as she handed her the cup of tea. "Was I crazy or did I pick up some kind of vibe between you two?"

Sage could feel herself flush and was grateful again for her Italian heritage. She could taste his mouth again on hers, feel the silky softness of his hair beneath her fingertips. "You have a much more vivid imagination than I ever gave you credit for."

She immediately wished she could call the words back, but to her surprise, Anna only laughed. "Sorry. Not much imagination here, but I do pride myself on my keen powers of observation. Comes from reading too many mysteries, I think."

"What did you see?" Sage asked warily.

"Wet handprints. They were all over his shirt. Unless the man has some kind of weird, acrobatic agility, I don't believe he could put handprints on his own back. And since you were the only one in the apartment with him, I guess that leaves you. Not that it's any of my business."

Sage could feel herself flush and for the life of her, she couldn't think how to respond.

"I hope this doesn't offend you," Anna went on, "but I have to tell you, he doesn't seem like your usual type."

"I wasn't aware I had a *type*."

"Of course you do. Everyone does."

She told herself she was grateful the conversation had turned from handprints—or anything else she might have put on Eben. "Okay, I'll bite. What's my type?

Anna added at least three teaspoons of sugar to her own cup as she gave Sage a sidelong look. "I don't know. Maybe some shaggy-haired, folk-singer guy who smells like patchouli and drives a hybrid with a Peace-Out bumper sticker on the back bumper."

She was too tired to be offended, she decided. Besides, she had to admit it was a pretty accurate description of the guys she usually dated. She sipped at her tea and grinned a little, astonished to find a sense of humor in Anna Galvez—and more astonished to find herself enjoying their interaction.

"All right, Ms. Know-it-All. What's your type, then?"

She was certain Anna's smile slipped a bit. "Well, probably not shaggy-haired folk singers."

Her evasion only made Sage more curious. She had never given much thought to Anna's social life, though she thought she remembered something about a broken engagement in the last few years.

"Seriously, are you dating anybody? Since we're living in the same house, it would be good to be prepared if I encounter some strange man on the stairway in the middle of the night."

Anna sighed. "No. I'm currently on sabbatical from men."

For some reason—probably because of her exhaustion—Sage found that hilarious. "Is there a stipend that goes with that?"

The other woman laughed and shook her head. "No, it's all purely gratis. But the benefits to my mental health are enormous."

No wonder Abigail had loved Anna. It was a surprising revelation in a day full of them, but by the time Sage finished her tea fifteen minutes later, all her misconceptions about Anna Galvez had flown out the window. The other woman wasn't at all the stuffy, serious businesswoman she presented herself as most of the time, at least the way she had always presented herself to Sage.

Why the facade? Sage wondered. Why had she always acted so cool and polite to her? Was it only a protective response to some latent, unconscious hostility Sage might have been projecting? She didn't want to think so, especially tonight when she was too tired for such deep introspection, but she had a feeling she may have been largely to blame for the awkwardness between them.

At least they had made this shaky beginning to building a friendship. They had a house and a dog and a life in common now. They should at least get a friendship out of the deal, too.

As the thought flickered through her mind, the scent of freesia seemed to drift through the room.

"Can you smell that?"

An odd look sparked in Anna's dark eyes and she set down her teacup. "I smell it all the time. It's like she's right here with me sometimes. But of course that's crazy."

"Is it?"

"I don't believe in ghosts. I'm sorry. I'm sure I'm a little more prosaic than you. I can't buy that Abigail still lingers at Brambleberry House."

"So what explanation do you have for it?"

Anna shrugged and spoke so quickly Sage was certain she must have given the matter some thought. "Abigail loved the smell of freesias. I think over her eighty years of living here and wearing the scent, some of it must have just absorbed into the walls and the carpet. Every once in a while, it's released by a shifting of molecules or something."

Sage wasn't convinced but she wasn't about to risk this tentative friendship by arguing. "Maybe," she answered. "I like it, whatever the explanation."

Anna smiled a little tremulously. "So do I."

"I should go. It's getting late." When Sage set down her teacup and rose, Conan didn't move from his spot curled up on his side by Anna's feet like a huge red foot-warmer. Apparently he was settled for the night. She felt a little twinge of jealousy but pushed it away. For some reason, she sensed Anna needed his company more than she did right now.

"I guess he's yours for the night."

"I guess."

"Good night. I, uh, enjoyed the tea."

Anna smiled. "So did I."

"Next time it's my treat."

"I'll count on it."

She said good-night to Conan, who slapped his tail against the floor a few times before going back to sleep, then she headed up the stairs to her apartment.

No freesia lingered in the air here, only the spicy scent of lasagna—and perhaps a hint of Eben's expensive cologne.

What was she going to do about the man?

Nothing, she answered her own question. What could she do? He would be leaving in a few days when his business here was done and she would go back to her happy, fulfilling life.

What other choice did she have? They were worlds apart in a hundred different ways. He was the CEO of a multinational corporation and she was a vegetarian nature-girl with a spooky, omniscient dog and a rambling old house full of ghosts and problems.

Yeah, the two of them seemed to generate this unlikely heat between them, but even if she were stupid enough to indulge herself by playing with it for awhile, dry tinder could only burn so long. Without the steady fuel of shared interests and emotional compatibility, the heat between them would probably flare and burn out quickly.

That thought depressed her more than it ought to.

She had a great life here in Cannon Beach, she reminded herself. Everything she could ever need. She knew that eventually this ache in her heart over losing Abigail would ease. She hurt a little less again than she had yesterday, a little less then than the day before that.

She would never stop missing her friend, but she knew eventually she would find her way back to homeostasis and begin to find happiness and joy in her life again.

Eben and Chloe Spencer would leave Cannon Beach in a few days and be just another memory. A pleasant one, yes, like all her many birdwatching hikes with Abigail and their hundreds of shared cups of tea, but a memory nonetheless.

"It's a good thing you're cute or I could definitely grow to loathe you for these morning tortures."

The object of her ire simply sat waiting by the door with an impatient scowl for Sage to lace up her running shoes. Despite spending the night in Anna's apartment, Conan must have squeezed out of his doggie door so he could come up the stairs and bark outside her door at the usual time to go running.

She yawned and tied her other shoe, dearly wishing she were back in her bed, that she had the nerve to send the mongrel down the beach to Eben's rental unit to drag him out of bed.

Since that conjured up too many enticing images of wavy dark hair against a pillow, of whisker-roughened skin and sleepy smiles, she jerked her mind back to Conan, who was quivering with impatience. He barked again and she sighed.

"All right, all right. I'm ready. Let's do this."

Conan bounded down the stairs of Brambleberry House, dancing around in the foyer in his eagerness to be gone as she followed more slowly, yanking her hair back into a ponytail as she went.

The morning air was cool and the rain had stopped sometime in the night, leaving wisps of fog to wrap through the garden and around the coastal pines beyond.

She stood on the porch stretching her hamstrings and listening to the distant sound of the sea and the call of that screech owl she'd heard the night before.

Maybe she didn't hate these runs with Conan after all, she decided. If not for them, she would miss all this morning splendor, simply for the sake of an extra hour of sleep.

The dog seemed wildly eager to go, whining impatiently and racing back and forth in the yard. Apparently he'd never heard of pulled muscles or torn ligaments, she thought sourly, then gave up stretching and followed him to the backyard, to the latched gate there that led directly to the beach.

The dog rushed out but Sage had to pause for a moment to prop the gate open so they could return that way instead of having to take a more circuitous route to the front of the house.

She straightened from the task and nearly collided with a solid wall of muscle.

"Oh," she exclaimed. She would have fallen if strong arms hadn't reached to keep her upright.

"Sorry," Eben murmured, heat flaring in his green eyes. "I thought you saw me."

"No. I wasn't paying attention."

After a moment's hesitation, he released her arm and she managed to find her footing as she caught sight of Conan a few yards away, racing around a giggling Chloe.

"Chloe! You're up early."

"Don't I know it." Eben looked at his daughter with disgruntled affection. "She woke me an hour ago, begging me to take her jogging with Conan this morning. We couldn't quite figure out the logistics, though. We didn't want to bang on your door at 6:00 a.m. just to pick up your dog, but then we saw your lights go on and headed over, hoping to catch you."

"Conan didn't give me a lot of choice this morning. He seemed particularly insistent on running today. Sometimes I think he's psychic. Maybe he knew you and Chloe were going to be here and wanted to make sure we didn't miss you."

"We came to take him running, so you can go back to bed," Chloe said with her guileless smile.

Tempting offer, Sage thought. That would certainly be the prudent course, to climb back into her bed, yank the covers over her head and pretend this was all a weird dream.

She couldn't do it, though. The morning was too lovely and she discovered she wasn't willing to relinquish the chance to be with them again, even though she knew it couldn't possibly be healthy for her.

"I've got a better idea," she said suddenly. "Come on inside to the garage for a moment."

Eben looked puzzled but he followed her and Chloe and Conan did the same. Sage quickly programmed the code to open the garage door. Inside she found one of Abigail's favorite toys propped against one wall and wheeled it out to where they waited for her.

Chloe's eyes widened when she saw Sage pushing the tandem bike out of the garage.

"Cool!" she exclaimed. "Is that yours?"

"It belonged to a friend of mine. We used to love to take bike rides together."

What a wealth of information that revealed about Abigail, she thought, that an independent woman in her eighties who lived with only an upstairs tenant for family would invest in a tandem bike. With her skill of gathering people around her, she never had a dearth of people to take rides with, from Will Garrett to Mr. Delarosa to the high school kids who delivered the newspaper.

"Can we ride it? You and me?" Chloe asked.

"I think that's a great idea. Your dad and that beastly dog can run if they want and get all sweaty and gross. We girls will enjoy a leisurely morning ride."

Chloe's glee nearly matched Conan's excitement. Sage glanced over at Eben and found him watching her with a murky look in his eyes that made her suddenly as breathless as if she'd just biked up the hill to Indian Beach.

It took Chloe a few moments to get the hang of the tandem bicycle, but by the time they made it a block, she was riding like a pro, giggling for the sheer joy of it.

Sage knew just how she felt. She wanted to laugh, as well. How could she ever have thought staying back in her apartment in bed would be preferable to this?

They stuck to pavement since she knew the soft sand of the beach would prove a challenge for Chloe. On impulse, she guided them south, away from town, with a specific destination in mind.

They encountered little traffic here this early in the morning. Conan and Eben ran ahead of them, Conan resigned to the leash. She had to admit, she enjoyed watching the play of Eben's muscles as he ran. Not a bad way to start the day, she decided.

She lifted her face to the pale streaks of sunlight shining toward the ocean. A strange emotion fluttered through her and it took her a while to recognize it.

She was happy, she realized.

For the first time since Abigail's death, she remembered what it was to savor life.

It was a gift, she decided, one she wasn't about to waste.

Chapter Nine

On a purely intellectual level, Eben knew he shouldn't be enjoying himself so much.

It was only a run, after all, just a brief interlude before he jumped right back into his normal routine of business calls and strategy sessions.

But the air was cool and sweet, his muscles had that pleasant burn of a good workout and the scenery was beyond spectacular, with the broad expanse of beach below them and the needles and sea stacks jutting into the sky offshore.

He wasn't sure where he was going, but Sage obviously had a destination in mind. Every once in a while she called out a direction—turn here, over that hill.

They continued to head south until they finally turned into a parking area with no cars in sight.

She parked the bike on the pavement, then led them down a short trail to a gorgeous, isolated beach, complete with an intriguing sea cave and gnarled, funky rocks.

He let Conan off the leash when they were away from the road and the dog and Chloe both jumped around in the sand with delight.

Sage watched them, the seabreeze playing in her hair.

"This is one of my favorite spots along the northern coast."

"I can see why."

"I like it not only for its beauty, but for its interesting history. It gives a rare glimpse into an earlier time."

"How?"

She led him to a rocky outcropping that looked as if it had been blasted through at one point. "See that? That was once a road carved into the headland there."

"A road?" Chloe asked. "For what?"

"Well, the highway we came here on wasn't built until the 1930s. Before then, this was the only way carriages and early cars could move up and down the coast, right on the beach."

For the next fifteen minutes, she gave them a guided tour of the place she called Hug Point. She pointed out many features Eben knew he wouldn't have paid any attention to had he been on his own and many more he wouldn't have understood even if he'd noticed them.

He was particularly fascinated by the stoplight still

embedded high on the rocky headland, more evidence of the beach highway.

"You have to be careful here, though," Sage said with a serious look. "The tide comes in faster than you expect. I have a friend who was trapped in the cavern for several hours by the tide and had to be rescued by the Coast Guard."

"I love it here." Chloe twirled her arms around, whirling across the sand with Conan barking alongside her.

Sage smiled at her with a soft affection that did weird things to Eben's insides. "I do, too. I think it's my favorite place on earth."

"Can we come back here tomorrow, Daddy?"

Eben wasn't quite sure how to answer. On the one hand, he hoped he could conclude his business with Stanley and Jade today and be back on his way to San Francisco by morning.

On the other hand, he hated the thought of leaving behind this smart, fascinating woman who made him feel things he never thought he would again.

"We'll have to see," he said, giving the classic parental cop-out. Chloe didn't seem to mind, especially when Sage picked up a piece of driftwood and tossed it far down the beach. An exuberant Conan bounded through the sand after it, then delivered it back, not to Sage but to Chloe. His daughter giggled and threw it again—not quite as far as Sage had, but far enough to make Conan work for it.

He and Sage stood some ways off and he was astonished again at the peace he felt with her.

He wasn't used to these moments of quiet. Usually his life was busy with troubleshooting and meetings and conference calls. Taking a few moments to pause the craziness, to focus only on breathing in sea air and savoring the morning, seemed healing in a way he wouldn't have expected.

He caught a glimmer of something in the sand and reached to pick it up—a baby-pink agate.

"Wow! That's really rare. Finding one is supposed to be lucky. Go ahead, make a wish."

He glanced at Chloe, too far down the beach with Conan to overhear them, then spoke with heartfelt—though no doubt unwise—honesty. "Okay. I wish I could kiss you again right now."

She froze and sent him a quick, startled look. Heat flashed there for a moment but she quickly veiled it. "Probably not a good idea."

"On several levels," he agreed. "I'll give it to Chloe and let her make the wish."

They were quiet for several moments as they watched the delighted dog and equally delighted child romp across the sand.

"Did you say you expect to be done with The Sea Urchin purchase in a few days?"

It was an obvious play to change the subject but he didn't argue. They were both probably better off pretending to ignore this heat they seemed to generate.

"I have to be," he answered. "I'm due in Tokyo by Tuesday of next week."

She gave him a piercing look as she pushed a strand of wind-tossed hair out of her face, tucking it behind her ear. "Are you planning to take Chloe along?"

He couldn't contain a little shudder at the idea of letting Chloe loose in a foreign country. The havoc she could wreak boggled his mind.

"While we're here enjoying the beaches of Oregon, my assistant has been busy interviewing new nanny applicants. She e-mailed me with the names of a couple of possibilities. I'll try to choose one when we return home this weekend."

He wasn't completely surprised to see storm clouds scud across her dark-eyed gaze. She stopped stock-still on the sand and stared at him.

"Let me get this straight. You're going to dump your daughter on a stranger picked by your *assistant* while you go out of the country?"

Despite her deceptive calm, she certainly knew just how to raise his hackles and put him on the defensive.

"I said I was choosing the nanny. My assistant is merely offering me a list of possibilities."

"Are you planning on actually meeting any of these worthy applicants before you fly out of the country and leave your daughter with them?"

"Yes. I'm not completely irresponsible, contrary to what you apparently think."

"But you won't stick around to see how she gets along with Chloe?"

"My plans can't be changed at this late date."

"So why don't you just take her and the new nanny with you?"

"Haul Chloe halfway across the world to Tokyo so she can sit in a hotel room with a stranger for a week?"

"Why not? At least then she wouldn't feel completely abandoned. You're the one stable thing in her life right now. You're all she has, Eben. Can't you see that?

"Of course I see that!" He was astonished how quickly his own much-vaunted calm seemed to be slipping away with the tide. "I live with the responsibility of it every moment of my life. I love my daughter, Sage, despite what you might think."

"I know you do. I can see it. But I'm just not sure Chloe is quite as convinced."

"What do you mean? I've never given her any reason to doubt it." At least he didn't think so.

"Children are resilient and bend with the wind like that seagrass over there, but they're not unbreakable, Eben."

"I have to go to Tokyo next week. Taking her along sounds perfectly reasonable in theory. But have you ever tried to keep an eight-year-old happy on a ten-hour flight?"

"I'm sure it's not easy. But isn't your daughter's sense of emotional security worth a little inconvenience?"

"It's more than inconvenience! It's impossible."

"Nothing is impossible for a man like you. You have the money and the power and the resources at your disposal to make anything happen. You just have to want to make it work."

He started to lash back at her—what the hell did this

do-gooder know about his life?—then he took a good look at her. She was angry with him, unquestionably, but there was something else in her eyes, something deeper. An old hurt he couldn't begin to guess at.

He opened his mouth to ask why this seemed so important to her. Before he could formulate the words, Conan raced to them, with the driftwood in his mouth, and dropped it at their feet.

He was followed immediately by Chloe, wind-whipped color on her cheeks and her hand outstretched.

"Look at this cool thing I found. What is it?"

He was fascinated to watch Sage inhale and exhale a long breath and then pick up the item in Chloe's hand. "Cool!" she exclaimed, with no trace of hurt or anger in her voice. "That's a little piece of petrified wood. You and your dad are great at beachcombing. He found a baby-pink agate. Maybe he'll let you make a wish on it."

"Oh, may I, Daddy?"

Grateful he hadn't tossed it back in the sand, he dug it from the pocket of his Windbreaker and handed it to her. She screwed her eyes shut for a moment, her mouth moving with words he couldn't understand, then she opened her mouth and handed it back to him.

"What did you wish?"

"Not telling. Then it won't come true."

"Fair enough. We should probably be heading back."

Chloe shook her head. "I want to keep looking for cool stuff on the beach."

"It's getting late," he insisted after a quick look at his watch. "Nearly a quarter to seven."

"No!" she said hotly. "I'm going to find more shells!"

He should have picked up on the signs. Chloe had been up for several hours already and was overstimulated by the excitement of the bike ride and playing hard with Conan. But she'd been on such good behavior in Sage's presence that her recalcitrance took him completely by surprise.

"Maybe we can make time later to look for shells, but we already have to hurry so you and Sage aren't late at the center."

"Not later! Now!"

"Chloe, get back here, young lady!"

Instead of obeying, she ran farther down the shore, coming dangerously close to the cold Pacific waters.

He headed after her, but the closer he got to her, the faster she ran, sending backward glances over her shoulder.

He saw truculence and defiance in her gaze, all the things he had become accustomed to seeing there the last two years. Though he tried to hang on to his temper, it was fraying already from his argument with Sage and he could feel it slipping through his fingers.

"Chloe Elizabeth Spencer, get your behind back here right now," he ordered. "You're in serious trouble."

"I don't care! I want to find more petrified wood."

And Sage thought he should subject the good citizens of Tokyo to Chloe?

He wouldn't put it past her to cause some kind of international incident and get them both thrown out of Japan.

He was within a few yards of grabbing her and tossing her, shrieking like a banshee, over his shoulder when Sage suddenly rode up on the tandem bike. He had no idea how she'd retrieved it from the parking lot so quickly or how she maneuvered it with such ease across the soft sand. He only knew he'd never been so grateful to see anyone in his life as he was to see Sage placidly pedaling toward them.

"Come on, Chloe. I need help getting back across the sand," she said calmly.

His daughter paused, still poised for flight but with a confused look on her features, as if she didn't quite how to react. "I want to find more petrified wood."

"I'm sure you do. But I'm afraid if we don't leave now, you and I will both be late for nature camp. Today I promised we were going to Ecola and Indian Beach, remember? I'm sure you'll find all kinds of shells there. You wouldn't want to miss it, would you?"

After a moment's reflection, Chloe shook her head and climbed onto the bicycle seat behind Sage.

"We'll have to use all our muscles to get across the sand. It's hard work. Are you ready?"

"Ready!" Chloe exclaimed, all signs of defiance miraculously gone.

Frustration simmered through him as Eben watched them work to pedal back toward the trail to the parking lot.

Even strangers were better at dealing with his

daughter than he was. He was far too reactionary, far too quick to let her push his buttons. She knew just how to make him lose his temper and she didn't hesitate to push her advantage.

Perhaps sending her to boarding school to learn control would give him at least a semblance of the upper hand in their relationship.

"Are you coming?" Sage asked at the parking lot. With a sigh of defeat, he nodded and jogged toward them.

The trip back toward town wasn't nearly as pleasant as the trip away from it. Conan seemed to be the only one enjoying himself, even with the leash he obviously despised firmly attached to his collar.

Sage seemed pensive and Chloe sulked while pedaling along on the back half of the bike.

Eben was almost glad they were all working harder to go back uphill. He didn't have the breath left to make conversation, even if he'd been able to find the inclination.

He wouldn't have expected it earlier in the morning, but he was relieved when they finally reached Brambleberry House.

"Why don't you take the bike the rest of the way back to your beach house?" Sage asked. "You'll get home faster on it. Perhaps you can find time to use it tonight or tomorrow to see some sights around town if you're still here. You can just drop it back here on your way out of town."

He didn't like thinking about saying good-bye, despite their earlier conflict and the inevitability of their parting. "Thank you," he answered. "And thank you also for the inside tour of Hug Point. It was nice to have our own private naturalist."

"You're very welcome."

She mustered a smile that didn't quite reach her eyes. In the widening sunlight, she looked lovely—fresh and untamed, her honey-gold hair slipping from its ponytail and curling riotously around her face, her cheeks flushed from the wind and the exercise.

"Bye Sage," Chloe chirped. "I'll see you in a while."

Sage waved to them as they took off down the road. Eben, busy with figuring out a tandem bike for the first time, could spare only one quick look behind him. She was watching after them, one hand on her dog, the other in her pocket.

Was that sadness he saw in her eyes? he wondered. He didn't have time to look closer, since he had to turn his attention to the road in order to keep both him and Chloe upright.

A curious ache caught in her throat as Sage watched them ride away on Abigail's bike. She told herself it was just because the fragile loveliness of the morning was ending. She had found unexpected pleasure in sharing the morning with Eben and Chloe, even the rough patch at the end.

She shouldn't have been so critical of his parenting. It had been presumptuous and rude and she winced now, remembering it. No wonder he had reacted so strongly.

Eben was not Tommy Benedetto, she reminded herself sharply. She was finding it far too easy to forget that, to project her own childhood and her father's emotional abandonment onto the dynamics between Eben and Chloe.

She had all but accused him of neglect. She supposed she needed to find a way to apologize to the man.

Conan barked what sounded suspiciously like agreement and settled at her feet, for all appearances completely worn out from the morning run.

She sighed. She was becoming entirely too wrapped up in the lives of two strangers she likely would never see after a few more days. Still, she couldn't help wishing she could find a way to help Eben see how very much his daughter needed him.

The strength of her desire took her by surprise. Gathering strays had been Abigail's specialty, not Sage's.

She had many friends in town but she had no misconceptions about herself. Most of her friendships were casual, superficial. She didn't allow people into her life easily. She wasn't standoffish or rude—at least she didn't think she was—but she was uncomfortable letting people see too deeply into her psyche.

Those protective instincts had been learned early at the prestigious boarding school she'd been sent to when she was around Chloe's age, around the time her father's new wife decided she didn't like competition for Thomas's attention.

At school, Sage had been immediately ostracized, marginalized. The stench of new money had clung to her—an insurmountable obstacle, especially since it was new money obtained only through her father marrying it.

She didn't want to think those years had shaped the rest of her life, but she couldn't deny that she was as cautious as a hermit crab about letting people too close to her.

What was different about Eben Spencer and his gamine little daughter? Already she cared about them and she couldn't quite figure out how it had happened so quickly. They were transitory in her life, she knew that, yet in only a few days they had both become dear to her—so dear she wanted to do all she could to smooth their path.

Maybe she had inherited that from Abigail, along with a rambling old house and a mongrel of a dog.

"Everything okay out here?"

She glanced up at the front porch to find Anna just leaving the house, dressed in a black pinstriped suit with a leather briefcase slung over her shoulder.

Neat and orderly, with her dark hair pulled back into a sleek chignon, she made Sage feel frumpy and sweaty. Big surprise there. She *was* frumpy and sweaty.

Anna also looked worlds different from the soft, approachable woman who had shared tea with her the night before.

"It's fine," she finally answered. "Just woolgathering for a moment but I suppose I'd better get moving if I want to have any chance of making it to work on time."

"Since Conan was gone when I woke up, I figured

he was with you. Looks like you've been out early this morning."

"He doesn't give me a whole lot of choice some days. It's hard to roll over and go back to sleep with him barking outside my apartment. I'm not sure which is worse, his insistent call outside the door or his big wet nose nudging me out of bed."

Anna grimaced. "I'm sorry. I've been letting you carry most of the burden for taking care of him and it's not fair to you. I'll take my turn tomorrow on the morning run."

"I complain about it but I don't really mind," she said quickly, and realized it was true. Somehow over the last month she had come to enjoy their solitary mornings.

"Well, I'll take a turn sometime, I promise. And don't worry about him this afternoon, either. I've got meetings this morning for my new store in Lincoln City and I should be home early."

She stared. "You never told me you were opening a store in Lincoln City. I had no idea."

Beneath her trim exterior, Anna brimmed with suppressed excitement. "The grand opening is in two weeks. We were trying to have it ready before the summer tourists started showing up, but we didn't quite make it."

"If it's opening by mid-June, you'll hit most of the high season, anyway."

"That's the plan."

Anna was quiet for a moment then she sighed. "I'm scared to death," she admitted.

Sage had a feeling that kind of raw truth was something the brisk, in-control Anna didn't share with many people and it warmed her to know Anna trusted her with it.

"Are you crazy? By-The-Wind rocks here in Cannon Beach. You're always busy. The new store will be great."

"I know, but we're entering a whole new demographic in Lincoln City. I've done the market studies and it looks like it will be feasible, but you never know what's going to click with people. Entering a new market is always a risk."

"If anyone can handle it, you can."

Anna look surprised, then pleased. "Thanks. That means a lot." She paused. "Everything has been so overwhelming the past month, with Abigail's death and the house and everything. If I could postpone the opening of the new store for a few weeks until I find my feet again, I would, but this has been planned for months. I don't have any choice."

No wonder Anna seemed so stressed and stiff all the time. Sage regretted again her rudeness, the deliberate distance she had imposed between them.

Eben and Chloe weren't the only ones she was letting deeper into her life, she realized. She was coming to consider Anna a friend as well.

Somehow she suspected that was exactly what Abigail had intended.

Chapter Ten

"Did everybody have fun at Ecola?" Sage asked the thirteen tired, sweaty children gathered around her at the end of the day.

"Yeeeessss!" came the resounding cheer from the campers.

"I did, too. Remember, if the weather cooperates, tomorrow is our beach day. We're going to spend the whole day on Cannon Beach, so make sure you have your hats and your sunscreen and a warm jacket. We'll be tide-pooling near Haystack Rock, flying kites and having a sand-castle competition."

She smiled as the campers cheered with excitement. "Now your parents will be here in a few moments. It's time to gather up your backpacks and the projects we did today so you're all ready to hit the road."

The campers jumped up and dispersed to the classroom where they stowed their gear. As she helped find missing jackets and refereed arguments over whose watercolor of aggregating anemone was better, she was aware of the anticipation curling through her.

Your parents will be here in a few moments, she had told the children, but it was the thought of only one parent's arrival that churned her pulse and sent wild-edged nerves zinging through her.

Ridiculous, she reminded herself.

Eben Spencer was just another parent and that's exactly the way she had to treat him. She certainly should not have spent what seemed like the entire day remembering their morning together—his powerful muscles as he ran beside her toward Hug Point, his slow smile as he enjoyed the sunshine, his low words when he said he wished he could kiss her again.

Even though they had argued, she couldn't seem to stop thinking about him.

She needed a good dousing in the Pacific.

Perhaps if she had seen him when he dropped off Chloe in the morning she wouldn't feel this glittery anticipation, but she had been busy on the phone arranging a field trip for the next session of camp. By the time she emerged from her office, Chloe had been working with Lindsey and several of the other children in a gathering activity to identify different sea creatures and their typical habitat and Eben had been nowhere in sight.

"Sage! There you are! I've been trying to catch you all week."

She groaned at the perky voice ringing through the center. Damn Eben Spencer anyway! If she hadn't been so distracted by thoughts of him, she might have been able to employ her usual tactics to avoid Tracy Harder. Now she had nowhere safe to go.

"Hi, Tracy. How are you?"

The other woman beamed at her. "Just great. I got the listings for two new properties today, right next to each other in Manzanita. They're half a block from the ocean and ought to move fast. So how were my two little terrors?"

She forced a smile. Tracy had been bringing her twins to camp for three years, ever since they turned old enough to attend, and right around the time their parents divorced.

The boys *were* terrors but she liked to chalk it up to high energy, not maliciousness.

"We had a great day today. I tried to keep them too busy to get into trouble."

"You are amazing with them, Sage. Thanks for putting up with them every year. I just wish you had camp year-round. I'd pull them out of school in a heartbeat and sign them up to every session."

Sage managed to contain a slight shudder. Fortunately, Tracy didn't require an answer before she went on. "So, let's talk," she said abruptly. "Brambleberry House."

Though she mentally groaned, she managed to keep a polite expression. "We've had this discussion already, Tracy. Several times. And nothing has changed at all since the last time we discussed it. I'm sorry, but Anna and I aren't selling."

"You two are crazy! Do you realize how much I can ask for a fifteen-room mansion on the beach? The place is a gold mine! With a little creative investment, you and Anna could be set for life."

"We can't do that, Tracy. I'm sorry, but Abigail would have hated to see us sell it."

"Abigail is not the one who will have to deal with all the repairs and the property taxes and the gigantic utility bills. Do you want to be tied to that house for the rest of your life?"

She had a brief, stark image of living forever in her turret apartment, growing old like Abigail, alone except for a big furry red dog who had been rescued from the pound.

A week ago, she would have found that image comforting. She wanted nothing more than to emulate Abigail, to be as feisty and independent as her friend for the rest of her days.

She wasn't sure what she wanted anymore. Her old childhood dreams of having a family of her own, born out of empty loneliness, had somehow re-emerged.

"You need to think long and hard about this," Tracy pressed. "I know you're still grieving for Abigail—we all are—but you're a young, beautiful woman. Trust me, someday you're going to want options."

She opened her mouth to answer but Tracy cut her off. "I've got a couple of Portland clients looking for a property for a bed and breakfast in town. Brambleberry House would be perfect. They have money to spare and I'm sure we could push the asking price well into seven figures. Talk to Anna about it. You have to!"

Sage shook her head. "No, Tracy. We're not selling."

The other woman's attention suddenly caught at something in the doorway, at the same time a tiny shiver skittered down Sage's spine.

Tracy's eyes widened and she let out a long breath. "Oh. My. Word. Who's the yummy guy? No, don't turn around."

She didn't need to turn around to know who it must be. Since this session of camp contained mostly local children, Tracy had to know all their parents—except one.

"How can I know who it is if you won't let me turn around to look?" she asked.

Tracy's eyes widened. "He's coming this way! Unless my eyes deceive me—and I don't think they do, trust me, I've got radar for these things—I can't see a ring. How's my hair?"

Sage studied her polished friend. Her makeup was perfect and not a strand of her highlighted blonde hair dared escape its trendy style.

In contrast, Sage didn't need a mirror to tell her what she must look like. Her dratted hair was probably falling out of the ponytail again, her skin felt tight and itchy, probably from a slight sunburn, and she didn't doubt she smelled as if she'd been chasing thirteen active elementary school students all day.

She sighed. "You look beautiful, as always."

"Liar!" Tracy purred, then her white teeth widened and she thrust out a hand, complete with the French manicure Sage knew she drove to Astoria to get and no trace of a callus or wrinkle.

"Hi there. I don't believe we've met. I'm Tracy Harder with Harder Realty. Welcome to Cannon Beach! Are you a summer visitor or are you moving in? Before you answer, let me just say how much I sincerely hope it's the latter. We just love new faces around here, don't we, Sage?"

"Uh, sure."

Eben blinked a few times at her gushing warmth, but finally held out his hand. "Hello. Eben Spencer. I'm afraid my daughter and I are only here until the weekend."

Tracy's face fell and she didn't look like she wanted to let go of his hand, as if she could change his mind just with her force of will. Eben finally managed to slip it away.

"Too bad for us. But if you ever think about moving back permanently, give me a call. Let me give you my card. Now you hang on to that, promise? I have listings up and down the northern/central coast, from Astoria to Newport. From luxury beachside houses to small two-room cottages, I can hook you up with anything you want. Anything."

Sage certainly didn't mistake the intent in that single, flirtatious word and Eben obviously didn't either.

"Uh, thank you."

"Oh, you're welcome. For instance, I just picked up two new listings today in Manzanita. The master suite in one of them is huge with one full wall of windows overlooking the ocean. Truly stunning and it's listed at several thousand dollars below appraisal. At that price, it's not going to last long. And the other one has four bedrooms, including one that would be perfect for an in-law suite."

Before Tracy could get revved up into a full-scale sales pitch, Sage took pity on Eben's glazed expression and stepped in. "Mr. Spencer, I imagine you're probably looking for the hiking trail guides we talked about this morning, aren't you?"

He looked baffled for only half a second, then seized on the excuse. "Yes. Exactly. I'm very anxious to see the area."

"I'm sorry, I meant to have them ready for you when you arrived to pick up Chloe, but it's been a rather busy day. It won't take me a second to dig them out of my files, though. They're back in my office, if you want to come with me. Tracy, will you excuse us?"

Tracy opened her mouth to object, but Sage didn't give her a chance, she just led Eben through the center to her office.

"Trail guides?" he murmured when they were safely out of earshot.

"I couldn't think of anything else. Sorry. Tracy's a sweetheart but she can be a bit of a piranha if she smells fresh meat."

He raised an eyebrow and Sage could feel herself flush. "Completely in the real estate sense of the word, I mean. Potential customers."

"Right."

He looked tired, she thought. His shirtsleeves were rolled up, his tie loose and that hint of disreputable stubble was back on his jawline. No wonder Tracy went into hungry mode.

"Uh, long day?"

He shrugged. "We're having some labor issues with a couple of our European properties. It took some serious negotiations, but I think we've finally got a handle on it."

He studied her for a long moment, a light in his eyes that left her suddenly breathless. "How about you?"

"It's been a good day. The kids seemed to enjoy Ecola. What's not to love? The place looks prehistoric, like dinosaurs will come stalking through the plants any minute now."

"How was Chloe today?"

"Tired, I think."

"I suppose that's what happens when she wakes us both up before five o'clock."

"Probably. She was a little bit cranky, but we didn't have any real problems. She fell asleep for a few moments in the van on the way back."

"She'll probably zonk out right after dinner, which will be good since I'm suddenly slammed with paperwork my assistant sent by courier."

She had a sudden fierce longing to run a finger down the tired lines at the corner of his mouth, as if she could soothe them. The impulse appalled her. "And are you the proud owner of a certain Cannon Beach landmark yet?"

"Not yet. They're stalling with every possible tactic they can come up with."

"Yet you're not giving up?"

He sighed. "I don't know. At this point, I'm not sure what else I can do. I can't force Stanley and Jade to sell, nor would I want to."

"Someone unscrupulous probably could figure out a way to do just that."

To her surprise, hurt flickered in his gaze. "Is that what you think of me?"

She considered the idea then rejected it. "Not at all. I think you're very determined but I don't believe you're ruthless."

"We need The Sea Urchin. I'm afraid nothing else will do."

"You need it or you want it? Big difference, Eben."

"Both. The more time I spend in Cannon Beach, the more I know this is the ideal location for another Spencer Hotel. It's perfect."

Before she could answer, Chloe skipped in and threw her arms around Eben's waist. "Hi Daddy. What are you doing in here?"

"Just talking to Sage."

She seemed to accept that with equanimity. "I'm

hungry. Can we have dinner at Brambleberry House again tonight?"

Eben looked taken aback at Chloe's question and sent a swift look toward Sage. Her first inclination was to go ahead and extend the invitation Chloe was angling for in her not-so-subtle manner, but she quickly checked the impulse. Eben said he had paperwork to finish.

Beyond that, she needed a little space and distance from the two of them to see if she could rebuild the protective barriers around her heart.

She forced a smile to Chloe. "I'm sorry, honey, but I've got other plans tonight."

It wasn't a lie. She was supposed to have her monthly book club meeting at By-The-Wind tonight, though all day she had been planning to do her best to wiggle out of it.

"What about tomorrow?" Chloe asked.

"We'll have to see," Eben stepped in. "Come on, Chloe. We'd better get out of Sage's hair and it looks like you need to get cleaned up before dinner. What do you say to pizza tonight?"

"I say *yum*," Chloe chirped.

Sage walked them to the door of the center. "Bye, Chloe. Don't forget your hat tomorrow. Remember, it's beach day."

"I can't wait! Can we ride bikes again tomorrow morning while Daddy and Conan run and go to Hug Point?"

She'd had a tough enough time getting the image of Eben's muscles out of her head all day today. She didn't need a repeat performance in the morning. "Guess what? I get to sleep in tomorrow since Anna wants to take a turn running with Conan in the morning."

To her surprise, disappointment sparked in Eben's gaze but he said nothing about it. "Come on, kid."

"Bye Sage," Chloe said reluctantly. She hugged Sage then grabbed her father's hand and walked outside.

This was becoming a habit Eben had a feeling would be tough to break when they returned to San Francisco.

Early the next morning, Eben stood at the deck railing watching the ocean change color with the sunrise, from black to murky blue to a deep, rich green. He was coming to depend entirely too much on these moments of solitude, when he had the vast beach to himself, sharing it only with the occasional shore bird.

He had intended to sleep in at least until six, but he woke an hour before his travel alarm had been set to go off. Restless and edgy, he had opted to come out here and enjoy the morning.

The beauty of the Oregon coast had somehow seeped into him. Despite the frustration over The Sea Urchin, he felt calmer here than he had in a long time. Maybe since those rough last few months of his marriage.

He shifted. He didn't like dwelling on Brooke and all the ways he had failed her. The worst of it was that now he wasn't even sure when he had stopped loving his wife.

She had been a friend of his sister Cami's and he had known her since she was a girl. He had been her escort at her debutante ball, had dated her through college. Theirs had never been a grand passion, but in the early days at least it had been comfortable.

And then after Chloe was born, she had wanted so much more from him. She had become clingy, demanding. She had hated his work schedule, had resented the hours he spent rebuilding the company, then had started accusing him of a long string of affairs.

Her emotional outbursts had all seemed so much like his parents' marriage—with the exception that his father *had* been having affairs, buckets of them, and no one could ever have called Hastings Spencer a workaholic. Alcoholic? Yes. Workaholic? Not a chance.

The last few years of their marriage had been miserably unhappy and he had worked even more to avoid the tumult he hated so much at home. He imagined if Brooke hadn't died, they would have been well on their way to divorce by now.

And most of it had been his fault. He acknowledged that now. He had been consumed with proving he was *not* his father, that he had inherited nothing from his unstable mother. As a result, he had refused to fight with Brooke, had refused to show much emotion at all.

He had lived with that guilt for two years now. The past couldn't be changed. Perhaps it was time to let it go.

He watched a black oystercatcher hop down the shore and his muscles hummed with a fierce desire to be out there on the hard-packed sand running for all he was worth.

He couldn't leave Chloe sleeping alone inside their

beach house, so he had to be content with watching the daybreak from the sidelines.

He sipped his coffee, remembering the morning only a few days ago when Sage had taken it out of his hand and sent him off running with her dog. Had it only been a few days ago? It seemed like forever since he had returned to find her asleep on the couch, warm and tousled and sexy, and had stolen a kiss.

He jerked his mind away from the memory and focused instead on the day ahead. He was meeting with Stanley and Jade that afternoon, for possibly the last time. If they still balked at the sale, he knew he would have to return to San Francisco and all the work waiting for him there. He couldn't linger here indefinitely, hoping he could change their minds.

He sighed, depressed at the realization that this would likely be his last Oregon sunrise for some time.

It was a glorious one, he had to admit. The sun coming over the Coast Range to the east tinted the sky above the ocean a pearly pink, with shades of lavender and pale orange.

Sage would love this.

He sighed. Couldn't he go five seconds without thinking about her? He was obsessed. He definitely needed to return to San Francisco soon so he could start shaking her from his mind.

As if in response to the direction of thoughts, he suddenly spied two shapes running down the beach, one of which was unmistakably a familiar shaggy red dog.

Anticipation curled through him and he knew with grim realization this was the reason he stood here at the railing—not to watch the sunrise, but on the off chance she might run past with Conan.

As they drew closer, he saw immediately his subconscious hope of seeing her would be dashed. Conan's companion didn't have unruly honey-gold curls. Instead, she had dark hair scraped back into a sleek ponytail.

Anna Galvez was taking her turn with the dog's morning run, just as Sage had told them the day before she planned to do.

The depth of his disappointment shocked the hell out of him.

How had a wild-haired nature girl become so important to him in a few short days? His fingers curled around the coffee mug. He should have done a much better job of keeping her out. What was the point of coming to care about her? He was leaving soon, tomorrow at the latest.

With sudden, hard dread lodged in his gut, he hated the idea of saying goodbye to her.

Conan barked an exuberant greeting and rushed over to his deck. Eben unlatched the gate and headed down the wooden stairs.

"Hey bud. No Chloe this morning. She's still sleeping." He scratched the dog's chin and was rewarded by furious tail-wagging.

Anna arrived several moments after the dog, panting hard. "My gosh, he's fast. I had no idea. Morning."

He smiled. "Good morning."

"How does Sage do this every morning? It's torture!" She straightened and he thought again that she was a remarkably lovely woman, with her glossy dark hair and delicate features.

He could appreciate her loveliness on a purely detached basis but he realized she did nothing for him. The realization was unsettling. He wasn't at all attracted to Anna Galvez—because all he could think about was Sage and her winsome smile and her untamed beauty.

"I guess you're the reason he insisted on dragging me in this direction," Anna said.

"Sorry."

She smiled. "I'm not. At least he's giving me a breather for a minute. Anyway, the ocean view is spectacular in any direction. I never tire of it."

"You're lucky to see it every day."

"I think so, too." She paused. "I never intended to stay here forever but I came a few years ago for a… vacation and I never left. I think seawater seeped into my blood or something. Now here I am a homeowner, a business owner. Settled. Life takes some strange twists sometimes."

He sensed there was more to her story, but didn't feel he knew her well enough to pry.

"I understand you may be joining the ranks of Cannon Beach property owners."

"Your mouth to God's ear."

She smiled again. "Will you be sticking around if you buy The Sea Urchin?"

Three days ago he would have given an unequivocal no to that question. The fact that he couldn't honestly offer her the answer he knew he should stunned him.

"Sorry. Not my business," she said, her voice somewhat stiff and he abruptly realized he must have been staring at her without speaking for several seconds.

"No, it's not that. I just don't quite know how to answer. Our hotel corporate office is in San Francisco, so I would have to say probably not. But I have a couple of great people in mind to run the place after we finish a few upgrades."

Conan barked and for some reason, Eben was quite certain that look in his eyes was disapproval. Did he need to consult a dog now on his business decisions?

"Well, Cannon Beach is a great place to raise a family if you should decide differently."

"I'll keep that in mind," he answered.

"Good luck with the Wus," she said. "I've read a little about Spencer Hotels and I think your company would treat The Sea Urchin exactly as it deserves."

"Thank you. Now if you wouldn't mind stopping at the hotel on your run and telling Stanley and Jade just what you told me," he joked, "maybe I could wrap things up here before Independence Day."

She laughed. "I'm not sure they'd listen to me. I've only been here three years so I'm still very much a newcomer."

Conan suddenly wriggled away from Eben and started heading up the beach. Anna gave a rueful smile. "I guess that's the boss's way of telling me it's time to head off. Thanks for giving me a chance to catch my breath."

"No problem."

She waved and headed off after the dog.

Six hours later, Eben wished for a little of Anna Galvez's encouragement as he sat in the elegantly ap-pointed conference room of The Sea Urchin, frustration burning his insides.

He had been running his family's hotel company since he graduated from The Wharton School in his early 20s. The company's assets and reputation had in-creased exponentially under his command.

With a far-ranging strategic plan, he had worked as hard as he knew how, had sacrificed and planned and maneuvered Spencer Hotels to emerge from near-bank-ruptcy to its current healthy market share.

Through all the years of toil and negotiations, he had never felt as completely inept as he did right this moment, gazing at Stanley Wu's smooth, inscrutable features.

The man was harder to read than the framed Chinese calligraphy hanging on the wall above his head.

"Mr. Wu, I'm sorry, but I don't know what else you and Mrs. Wu want from me. I have tried to convince you Spencer Hotels doesn't plan any radical changes to The Sea Urchin. You've seen our business plan and the blue-prints for the minor renovations we would like to see. You have physically toured each of our two other hotels in Oregon as well as two in Washington and I've showed you multimedia tours of several others. I've given you my personal promise that I will treat this establishment with the same care and attention you and Mrs. Wu have showered on it for thirty-five years. I want this hotel, I've made no secret of that fact, but my time here is running out. What else can I do to convince you?"

Stanley studied him for a full minute without saying anything—an eternity, Eben thought. Finally Stanley's mouth lifted slightly in what Eben supposed passed for a smile.

"Come to dinner tonight. Seven o'clock. Bring your daughter."

Eben gave a mental groan. Of all the things he might have expected, that was way down at the bottom of his list. It was also the one thing he did *not* want to do. The way things were going, Chloe would pitch a fit and destroy any chance he had of making this deal.

This was one more hoop the Wus were making him jump through. Perhaps one too many.

"I don't know if that's a good idea. Chloe's only eight. Her manners are not exactly what you might call impeccable."

"Bring her," Stanley said sternly. "My father used to say, if you want to know the health of the tree, study the fruit."

Eben had to fight to keep from banging his head on the conference table a few times as he felt his chances for buying The Sea Urchin slipping through his fingers like sand.

This was a certifiable nightmare. His entire plans—all the months of study and work—hinged on the table manners of a moody, unpredictable eight-year-old girl.

He should just tell the man to go to hell. Eben had worked harder on this deal than anything in the dozen years since he took over at the helm of Spencer Hotels. If it wasn't enough for Stanley Wu, so be it.

Even as he opened his mouth to tell the man to forget the whole thing, something stopped him.

"Of course," he found himself murmuring instead, at the same moment a germ of an idea sprouted.

He thought of Chloe a few nights before at dinner, how polite and patient she had been while they ate vegetarian lasagna at Brambleberry House. If he could somehow replicate that behavior, there was a tiny—miniscule—chance he might pull this off.

Sage's presence had made all the difference. She had some uncanny moderating effect on Chloe's misbehavior. If she could distract his daughter long enough, convince her to behave for one simple evening, perhaps all hope was not completely lost.

"Do you mind if I bring along a guest?" he asked before he gave himself time to think it through.

Stanley studied him across the conference table. "What guest is this?"

How exactly did he explain? "My daughter and I have befriended a Cannon Beach resident, Sage Benedetto. I would like to bring her along, if it would be acceptable to you and Mrs. Wu."

This time the cool look in the other man's eyes was replaced with the first genuine smile Eben had seen there. "Ah. Sage. Yes. A beautiful woman always improves the digestion."

"More wisdom from your father?"

Stanley laughed. "I don't need my father to tell me this truth. I have eyes, don't I?"

"Uh, right."

"So you will come for dinner and bring your daughter and our friend Abigail's beautiful wild rose, yes?"

"Yes," he answered.

Now he just had to convince Sage.

Chapter Eleven

"Now remember, what's the most important tide-pool rule?"

"Look but don't touch!" the six campers in her group recited as one and Sage beamed.

"Exactly right. The rocky shore ecosystem is very fragile and you never know what harm you could do even by picking up a piece of kelp. It's much better just to take pictures and look. All right, everybody grab your disposable cameras and let's start recording our observations."

The kids broke off into their pre-assigned teams of two and, chattering with excitement, headed on their field assignments to record as many tide-pool creatures as they could find.

Sage watched their eager faces and had to smile. This was close to her idea of a perfect day. The sun, making a brief appearance between storms, was bright and warm on her face, the water a spectacularly beautiful shade of deep olive. She had a bright group of children soaking in knowledge like little sea sponges.

For the next half hour, she wandered through the three teams, answering questions, making observations, pointing them toward species they may have missed: tiny porcelain crabs and Hopkin's roses.

She loved it out here. She didn't need anything else, certainly not any sharp-eyed executives who smelled like heaven and kissed like a dream.

She pushed thoughts of Eben away—again—and focused on the tide-poolers until her stopwatch beeped, then she gathered them around to compare notes.

"Excellent job, all of you. You're now official junior naturalists for Cannon Beach."

"Ms. B., when can we have the crab race? You promised you'd let me whip your butt this year."

She laughed at Ben Harder, one of Tracy's twins. "Excuse me, but I believe I promised I would let you *try* to whip my butt. Big difference there, kiddo."

"When? Can we do it now?"

She checked her watch. They had split the campers into two groups so they didn't stress the tide-pool residents with too much attention at once. Lindsey had the other group down the beach flying kites and they weren't due to switch places for another twenty minutes.

"Okay. Crab races it is. We need start and finish lines."

Two of the boys found a piece of driftwood and charted a race course of about thirty feet—far too long in Sage's book, but the children insisted they could go that far.

Her idea was for one-on-one races, but eventually everybody wanted to compete against her and it turned into a free-for-all.

It was a fight to the finish but she came in a respectable third—behind Ben Harder and Leilani Stein. At the finish line, panting and aching, she collapsed into the sand. How did she seem to forget every year until the first camp of the summer how blasted hard it was to walk backward on her hands and feet? It took her abs all summer long to relearn how to crab race.

"Good race," she said, gasping. "But I think you got a head start."

"No way," Ben exclaimed. "It was totally fair!"

"Need a hand up?"

At the low, masculine voice, Sage opened her eyes and found Eben standing over her, his hand outstretched.

Her heart gave a sharp kick in her chest at his features silhouetted in the sunshine. He looked gorgeous in a pair of khaki slacks and a casual cotton shirt.

Of course he would. She was hot and sweaty and probably smelled like a tide-pool again. She wanted to burrow into the sand like a geoduck clam. Instead, she released a tiny sigh, reached for his hand and let him help her to her feet.

"I have to say, the kid's right. It looked fair to me. If anybody jumped the gun, I think it was you."

She brushed sand off her butt. "Whose side are you on?"

He grinned and she forgot to breathe. She had no idea he could look so lighthearted. It was a disturbing revelation.

"Did you need Chloe?" she asked to cover her reaction. "Her group is down the beach. See the kites down there?"

"No. I saw them first and already stopped to talk to her," he answered. "Your assistant—Lindsey, I think is her name—told me I could find you out here."

Note to self, she thought, *remind Lindsey not to send gorgeous men out searching for me when I'm crab-walking in the sand.*

She pushed wind-tossed hair out of her face. "Is there some problem with Chloe?"

"In a way."

His temporary lightheartedness seemed to slide away again and he shifted a little, looking suddenly uncomfortable.

She had no idea what he wanted and he didn't seem in any big hurry to enlighten her. "Do you need me to keep her after camp ends again?" she said, hazarding a guess. "It's really no problem."

"It's not that." He let out a long breath. "The truth is, I need to ask a huge favor and I'm not sure quite how to go about it."

The kids in her group seemed happy enough with

continuing their crab races so she led him down the sand a little. "Just ask, Eben."

"You make it sound easy." He paused. "All right. Will you come to dinner at The Sea Urchin tonight?"

She gave a surprised laugh. "This is your huge favor? Inviting me to dine at the finest restaurant on the northern coast? By the tone of your voice, I was expecting you to ask me to donate a kidney or something."

"That might be less painful in the long run. The truth is, I need help with Chloe. Stanley has invited me to dinner tonight." He paused. "No, that's not right. There was no invitation involved. He *ordered* me to come to dinner tonight and to bring Chloe along. Apparently, before the man will make a final decision to trust me with his hotel, he wants to see how I interact with my daughter."

Sage flushed, embarrassed that she had initially allowed herself to feel flattered, to imagine he might have been asking her on a date. "And how do I fit into the picture?"

"You're so good with Chloe. With you, she's a different girl. She's polite and well-mannered. Happy. I need her to be on her best behavior and you seem to bring the best out in her where I seem to usually have the opposite effect."

It was ridiculous to feel this hurt that spread out from her stomach like the paralyzing venom of a jellyfish sting.

"So you're inviting me as your daughter's handler in order to help you clinch the deal?"

He winced. "Put like that, it sounds pretty damn nervy, doesn't it?"

"Yes," she clipped off the word.

"I'm asking you to help me for one night. This is important to me. You have the magic touch with Chloe. Everything seems to go more smoothly when you're around. Please, Sage. It's one night."

All her instincts cried out for her to tell him to go to hell. She thought of that kick in her heart when she first saw him. How ridiculous. She was allowing herself to have feelings for a man who only viewed her as a convenient caregiver for his daughter.

With every ounce of her, she wanted to tell him no. She even started to form the word, but her mouth seemed to freeze.

She couldn't do it.

He wanted The Sea Urchin desperately—he had made no secret of that—and she cared about him and about Chloe enough that some part of her wanted to help him reach his goal.

Four days ago she might have scoffed and told him to go back to his business meetings and his conference calls. But that was before she had come to know him.

The truth was, she had become convinced Spencer Hotels would be good for Cannon Beach and The Sea Urchin. Abigail must have thought so or she never would have suggested the idea. It seemed a betrayal of her friend to refuse to help Eben simply because some foolish part of her hoped he wanted more from her than etiquette lessons for his daughter.

"Please," he repeated.

She was going to bleed from a thousand gashes in her

heart when he and Chloe left. Helping him tonight would only accelerate that inevitable heartbreak. She knew it perfectly well, could already feel the ache, but from somewhere deep she still managed to dredge up a smile.

"What time?"

The pure delight on his face almost broke her heart right there. "Seven. Will that work for you?"

Her mind raced with the million things she would have to do between the time she finished work and seven o'clock. Foremost was the purely feminine lament that she had nothing to wear and no time to run to her favorite vintage boutique in Portland to find something.

"If Anna's home to stay with Conan, it should be fine."

He reached for her hands and she was certain if they weren't standing on a public beach in broad daylight with a hundred other people, he would have kissed her right then.

"My debt to you seems to grow larger by the minute. Somehow I'll find a way to pay you back, I swear it."

"Don't worry about it. I'll see you at seven."

"No, no, *no*!" Sage wailed, her breath coming in short gasps as she pedaled hard up the hill toward Brambleberry House. With one hand on the handlebars, she used the other to hold her umbrella over the dress that had just cost her an entire week's paycheck.

It was wrapped in plastic but she bemoaned every single raindrop that made it around the umbrella to splatter against her precious cargo. The whole dress was going to be ruined, she just knew it. Worse, her hair was drenched and would take hours to dry.

She had exactly forty-five minutes to ride the half-mile home and to shower and primp for her dinner with Eben and Chloe and the damn pouring rain wasn't making this any easier.

She could barely see and didn't have a spare hand to wipe the rain out of her eyes and she lived in mortal dread her tires were going to slip in the mud at the shoulder of the road and dump her *and* the dress.

A vehicle drove slowly past and she shifted the umbrella over the dress until it was almost vertical like a warrior's shield, just in case the driver hit a puddle and splattered it everywhere.

Instead, the vehicle slowed even further, then she saw brakelights through the rain. She could barely make out that the truck belonged to Will Garrett until the driver's door opened and he climbed out.

"Get in," he called. "I'll throw your bike in the back of the truck and drive you the rest of the way home."

"I'm almost there."

"Get in, Sage. It's not safe for you to be riding your bike in these conditions. It's slick and visibility is terrible, though I have to say, the bright pink umbrella does tend to draw the eye."

She winced at the ridiculous picture she must make. "I bought a fancy new dress. I didn't want it to get wet."

Will's eyes widened, but to her relief, he said nothing as he took the bicycle from her and effortlessly lifted it into the back while she rushed to open the passenger door. Inside the cab, she laid her dress carefully on the bench seat then climbed in behind it, closing her vivid umbrella.

Will's heater blared full force and she relished the warmth seeping into her chilled muscles for the few moments before he joined her and pulled back onto the road toward Brambleberry House.

"Do I dare ask what's up with the dress? It's not your usual kind of thing, is it?"

She could feel her face flame. "I'm having dinner at the Sea Urchin tonight and it occurred to me I don't have a lot of grown-up clothes to wear. I splurged a bit."

She glanced at it, a sleek midnight blue dream of a dress shot through with the barest trace of iridescent rainbow thread. *Splurge* was a bit of an understatement. She had spent more on this one dress than she usually spent on clothes all year long. Her Visa balance would probably never recover.

It had been purely an impulse buy, too. She hadn't really intended a whole new dress. Since she couldn't make it to her favorite shop in Portland, she thought she would only take a quick look at some of the local stores on the off chance she might find a blouse on clearance she could wear with her usual black dress skirt.

She had just about given up on finding anything when she wandered into a new shop and saw this dress hanging in a corner.

The moment she saw it, she had fallen in love, despite the hefty price tag.

"So what do you think?" she asked Will.

He smiled ruefully. "I'm the wrong guy to ask. Afraid I'm not the best judge of that kind of thing. Robin used to throw a fit because I usually didn't even notice when she bought something new."

He didn't often refer to his late wife or their life together and she could tell it still bothered him to do so because he quickly changed the subject.

"The Sea Urchin, huh? Hot date?"

If only. She burned with embarrassment again, remember her first conclusion when Eben asked her. "Not quite. I'm taking an eight-year-old. One of my day campers. Her dad is negotiating with Stanley and Jade to buy the hotel and he and his daughter have been invited to dinner. Eben, in turn, invited me. They're coming in exactly—" she glanced at her watch as they pulled into the Brambleberry House driveway "—forty minutes now."

"You'd better hurry then. Run in and put on your fancy dress. I'll put your bike away in the garage for you."

On impulse, she leaned across her dress and kissed his cheek, smelling sawdust and sweat, a surprisingly pleasant combination.

"Thanks, Will. I owe you. Come for dinner next week, okay?"

"As long as there's no tofu on the menu."

"I'll see what I can do."

She opened her umbrella, clutched her dress to her as if it were spun gold—a fair description, really, penny for penny—and dashed out into the rain.

She reached the porch just as Anna opened the door to let Conan out. The dog barked a greeting, but to her vast relief he didn't jump all over her in his usual away, almost as of the uncanny beast knew she didn't have time to play.

"That looks like something fabulous," Anna exclaimed, gazing at the dress. "Let's see."

Sage held it up, gratified by Anna's moan of appreciation.

"Gorgeous!" she exclaimed. "What's the occasion?"

"I'm having dinner at The Sea Urchin tonight with Eben and Chloe."

Anna gave her a careful look, then smiled. "Do you have any jewelry to match?"

Ha. After buying the dress, her budget barely stretched to a new pair of pantyhose. "I'll find something."

"Don't forget we have Abigail's whole glittery collection to choose from. Go get dressed and I'll bring her jewelry box up and see what we can dig out."

Sage raced up the stairs two at a time. This excitement pumping through her was only adrenaline, she told herself, just a normal reaction to her urgency and the ever-ticking clock.

She hadn't been on a date in a long time. Did this qualify, since Chloe would be along? Probably not. But she still couldn't shake the bubbling anticipation and she took the fastest shower on record.

She raced through her makeup—something she rarely bothered with—then took a page out of Anna's fashion book and pulled her still-damp hair into as smooth an updo as she could manage with her unruly frizz.

She had just slipped into the dress and was working the zipper when Anna knocked on the door.

"It's open. Come in," she called.

Anna's arms overflowed with Abigail's huge jewelry box, but all Sage focused on was the astonished admiration in her eyes.

"Wow. That's all I can say. Wow. That dress is perfect for you. The coloring, the style, everything."

"That's why I spent far more than I could afford on it. Stupid, isn't it, for a dress I'll probably only wear once."

"Every girl needs something completely, outrageously impractical hanging in her closet."

"I guess I'm covered, then."

"Not yet. Let's see what Abigail has in her magic box." She held out the jewelry box that contained what had been another of Abigail's passions—vintage costume jewelry, which she wore loads of at every opportunity.

Even when she worked in the garden, Abigail would wear some kind of gorgeous jeweled earbobs and a matching necklace.

"I need to glitter," she used to say with that mischievous gleam in her blue eyes. "It takes the attention away from my wrinkles."

To Sage's shock, Anna turned the box with its jumbled contents and upended the whole thing onto her bed.

The two of them stared at the huge sparkly pile for

a long moment. Sage hadn't given much thought to the collection, but now she couldn't seem to look away.

"Do you suppose any of it's real?" Sage whispered.

"I don't know." Anna spoke in the same hushed tone. "I'm not sure I *want* to know."

She started pawing through the collection, pulling out a gleaming strand of pearls here, a chunky citrine and topaz necklace there.

Finally she stopped and pulled out an Art Deco choker in stones the exact midnight shade of the dress. "This is it. It's perfect."

The stones felt as smooth and cool as polished sea glass. After another moment of treasure hunting, Anna pulled out a pair of matching dangly earrings that seemed to capture the light and reflect it back in a hundred different shades of blue.

"I guess we really should have this collection appraised," Anna said while Sage put them in.

"You don't sound any more enthusiastic than I am."

"They're Abigail's. I hate the idea of parting with *any* of her things. But let's face it, the upkeep on the house is going to be more than either of us can afford. The heating bill alone is almost as much as I was paying for rent on my condo."

"We'll figure it out."

"You're right. No depressing talk," Anna said firmly. "Let's just get you ready. We can worry about heating bills and extravagant jewelry collections another day."

Already Sage could feel her hair slipping out of the

style. Before the whole thing could fall apart, Anna fiddled with a few strands, smoothed a few more, then stepped back to admire her handiwork.

"All done. What do you think?"

Sage stared at her full-length mirror at the stranger gazing back at her. Not a stranger, she corrected. She only had a single picture of the slim, lovely mother she barely remembered, a picture rescued and hidden away when her father started to purge that part of his life after his second marriage.

She hadn't looked at it in a long time, but somehow she knew if someone snapped a picture of her right now and compared it with that precious photograph, the two women would be nearly a match.

Tears burned behind her eyelids, but she choked them back. "Oh, Anna. Thank you. The necklace and earrings are exactly right."

Anna stepped back and studied her. "It's almost spooky the way they match, as if Abigail bought them just to go with that dress."

Maybe because she had been thinking of her mother, but Sage could swear she felt invisible fingers gently brush her cheek.

She shivered a little and was grateful when the doorbell rang.

"There's Eben," she said, then felt ridiculous for the inanity. Who else would it be?

"Have a wonderful time," Anna said. "Give my love to Stanley and Jade."

"I will."

Anna looked bright and animated, Sage thought, so very different from the stiff businessman she had always considered her. She really was becoming a dear friend, something Sage never would have expected.

She reached out and gave Anna a quick, impulsive hug. "Thank you again."

Anna looked stunned but pleased. "You're very welcome. I'll go let him in. Wait up here a moment so you can make a grand entrance down the stairs."

"Oh, for heaven's sake. I'm not in high school."

"Trust me. Stay here."

Anna flew down the stairs and a moment later, Sage heard Eben's deep voice greeting her. She tried to count to twenty but only made it to fifteen before she started down the stairs, certain she was going to trip in the unaccustomed high heels and break her neck.

Eben stood at the bottom of the stairs waiting for her in a dark suit and tie. He looked sinfully gorgeous and she had to admit his thunderstruck expression more than made up for the sheer extravagance of the dress.

By the time she reached the bottom step, Anna was ushering Conan into her apartment and closing the door behind them both with one last delighted smile at Sage and Eben in the entryway.

Eben grabbed her hand and brought it to his mouth in a gesture that should have felt foolish but seemed exactly right.

"You look stunning," he murmured.

"I feel like I'm on the way to the prom."

He gave a surprised laugh. "I sincerely hope I've moved beyond the arrogant jackass I was at seventeen."

"Well, I have to admit my prom date didn't bring along his eight-year-old daughter."

"Left her home with a sitter, did he?"

She laughed at the sheer unexpectedness of his teasing. "Something like that."

"I should probably tell you, Chloe's over the moon about spending the evening with grown-ups. We had to rush out and buy her a new dress and everything."

Thank heavens they hadn't bumped into each other in the few Cannon Beach clothing stores. "The Wus have a dozen grandchildren. Trust me, they're going to adore her."

He drew in a deep breath, his eyes filled with doubt. "I guess we'll find out in a few moments, right?" He held out his arm. "Shall we?"

She slipped her arm through his. The rain forced them to stand close together and share his umbrella and she could smell the deliciously spicy scent of his aftershave.

This was a make-believe night, she reminded herself as he helped her into his luxurious rental car. She needed to remember that by morning this would all be a memory.

A wonderful, glorious, heartbreaking memory.

Chapter Twelve

"Mrs. Wu, this fortune cookie is delicious. I like it very much. Would you mind if I had a second one?"

Eben observed his daughter's careful politeness with amazement. What kind of well-mannered gremlin had snuck in when he wasn't paying attention and replaced his headstrong daughter with this sweet, polite little person?

He glanced over at Sage and caught her suppressing a smile.

Jade Wu only beamed at Chloe, her lovely, ageless features glowing with delight. "You have as much as you want, child. Fortune cookies are not really from China, did you know that?"

"I didn't know that. Really?" Chloe looked enthralled.

"They were invented right in your town of San Francisco by a smart baker at a Japanese restaurant. But our guests expect them, so we have perfected our own recipe."

"You make them here?"

Jade smiled at her. "They are not hard. I can show you how, if you would like."

Chloe's eyes widened with delight. "Oh, could you? That would be so cool! Can you show me now?"

Sage made tiny sound in her throat, enough that Chloe gave her a careful look, then moderated her glee to a respectful smile toward Jade Wu. "Only if it wouldn't put you to too much trouble, of course."

Jade looked as amused as Eben had ever seen her in their brief acquaintance. "Not at all. Not at all. I am certain we could find a good apron to put over your lovely dress."

"Thank you very much," Chloe said calmly but Eben could see her nearly vibrating with excitement.

He couldn't help breathing a huge sigh of relief. Chloe had been perfectly behaved all evening. She had been respectful of both of the Wus, had waited her turn to interject a comment or question and had used impeccable table manners.

He knew exactly who deserved the credit for the remarkable transformation—the stunning woman sitting beside him. Sage caught his gaze again and smiled in a conspiratorial way and his heart seemed to stutter in his chest.

Emotions tangled in his throat as he looked at her—tenderness and admiration and something else, something deeper he wasn't sure he could afford to examine closely.

"You should ask your father first, of course."

Chloe grabbed his hand and pressed it between both of hers in her dramatic way, as if she were pleading to save a life instead of only asking permission to bake a cookie. "Oh, please, may I, Daddy?"

"Of course, as long as Mrs. Wu doesn't mind showing you and you do exactly what she says."

She kissed his cheek and Sage smiled at him again. For some silly reason, Eben felt as if he had just hand-delivered the moon to both of them.

"Sage, would you care to come with us?" Jade asked her. "I will find an apron for you as well."

"I'd love to see how it's done," she answered. "But I believe I'll just watch, apron or not."

Eben rose when the three lovely females did and watched them head for the kitchen, Jade in the lead, leaving him alone with Stanley.

The other man didn't seem in any hurry to resume his seat even after the door closed behind the women, so Eben stayed on his feet as well. "Thank you for dinner. It was exceptional, as usual. Tonight, I especially enjoyed the duckling."

Stanley continued to study him out of impassive eyes. Just before the pause between them would have turned awkward, Stanley turned and headed away from the table. "Come with me, Eben Spencer."

Baffled and more than a little edgy, he followed Stanley to the suite of rooms that contained the hotel's administrative offices.

Stanley sat behind his elegantly simple desk and with a solemn look in his eyes he gestured for Eben to take a seat.

"My wife and I have loved this hotel," he said after a long moment. "It has been our home and our lives for many, many years. We have raised two strong sons here and had hoped one of them would choose to carry on for us, but our sons have chosen other paths to follow."

Eben wasn't quite sure where Stanley was steering the conversation so he opted to remain silent and let the man lead.

"My wife and I are old and we are tired. We spend so much time caring for those who stay here that we have no time to enjoy our older years. The moment has come for us to make a decision about the future of this place we love."

Eben held his breath, doing his best to contain the nerves shooting through him.

"I know you have been impatient with us for the delays. But I hope you understand how difficult it is for us to let go and surrender our dream to another. We needed to be certain. Completely certain. Tonight, seeing you with your beautiful daughter, we are sure of our decision. A man who could raise such a delightful child will take good care of this hotel, the child of our hearts."

The other man pulled out the file Eben knew contained the paperwork for the sale of The Sea Urchin to Spencer Hotels. He signed it in his small, neat script, then handed the papers over to Eben.

He had negotiated hundreds of deals in his dozen years at Spencer Hotels, but Eben couldn't remember any victory tasting as sweet as this one. He wanted to laugh out loud, to throw his fists in the air.

To find Sage and kiss her senseless.

She deserved every bit of credit for this. If not for her and her miraculous effect on Chloe, he wouldn't be sitting here watching Stanley Wu hand him exactly what he wanted, ownership of this graceful old hotel.

Instead of leaping up to go in search of Sage, he settled for holding his hand out across the desk to shake the other man's hand.

"Thank you, Mr. Wu. I give you my solemn vow that you will not regret this."

They would have to go through this again in the morning with attorneys present, but Eben knew Stanley would not change his mind now, not after he had given his word.

They spent several moments discussing a few of the myriad details involved in the sale. He tried his best to focus, but inside he couldn't wait to find Sage and tell her.

Stanley must have finally sensed his impatience.

"All this can wait until tomorrow with the lawyers. Tonight is for being with those we love," Stanley said, then paused. "Our Sage, I have never seen her looking so lovely."

An odd segue, he thought, rather discomfited. "Uh, right."

"And she is just as lovely on the inside. A man would be a fool to let such a rare and precious flower slip through his fingers."

Eben couldn't have said why this particular conversational detour left him slightly panicked. Would Stanley rip up the papers if Eben told him things weren't serious between him and Sage?

He searched the other man's features but could see nothing behind Stanley's serenity.

"Shall we join our women in the kitchen? I am always looking for good fortune."

Still feeling a bit off center, Eben followed Stanley into the kitchen. They stood in the doorway, admiring the lovely picture of women across three generations working together.

The delicious-smelling kitchen was busy and crowded as the head chef and his workers served the other dinner guests. Jade had taken over a workspace in the corner and was overseeing as Chloe and Sage— aprons tucked carefully over their dresses—folded thin circles of soft-cooked cookies into half-moons around little slips of paper, then curved and tucked them into the traditional fortune-cookie shape.

Chloe was laughing with delight as she worked, he saw, and so was Sage, her lovely features bright and animated.

He could barely look away.

Something shivered in his chest, a sense of rightness, of belonging, that had been missing for a long time.

She glanced up and for a tiny sliver of time, their

gazes locked together. Her smile slid away, her eyes suddenly as deep and fathomless as the Pacific.

He would be leaving her tomorrow. The grim knowledge churned through him and he suddenly hated the very thought of it. But what other choice did he have?

Chloe caught sight of him. "Daddy, come and see my fortune cookies! I made one just for you. I even wrote the fortune and put it inside and everything."

He jerked his gaze away from Sage, from that stunning, tensile connection between them, and smiled at the cookie in her outstretched hand. "Thanks, kiddo. It's too pretty to eat, though."

"But if you don't eat it, you won't get to see the message."

Four sets of eyes watched him as he broke open the cookie and pulled out the folded slip of paper inside. He unfolded it, only to find Chloe's girlish handwriting, much tinier than usual, was almost indecipherable.

With effort, he was finally able to read the message aloud. **To the best Daddy ever. I love you better than all the fortune cookies in the world.**

To his complete astonishment—and no small amount of dismay—tears welled up in his eyes. Eben blinked them back rapidly, shoving them down as far as he could into his psyche.

"It's great," he said brusquely when he trusted his voice again. "Thank you very much."

Chloe was obviously looking for more from him. Her features fell. "You don't likc it."

"I do." He tried a little more enthusiasm. "I love it. The cookie tastes great and the fortune is...well, it's not true."

Now she looked close to tears. "It is *too*. I do love you more than all the fortune cookies in the world."

He would have preferred this conversation anywhere else than in the busy, noisy kitchen of the hotel he had just agreed to buy—and anywhere else but in front of Stanley and Jade Wu and Sage Benedetto. "I know you do, sweetheart. I just meant the first part isn't true. I'm far from the best daddy in the world, but I'm trying."

She smiled her relief and threw her flour-covered hands around his waist. "Well, I think you're the best."

He hugged her back. "That's the important thing, then, isn't it?"

He had won. The Sea Urchin was his.

Neither Eben nor Stanley mentioned the matter for the rest of the evening. Even after the three of them took their leave of the Wus, Eben didn't say anything, but Sage somehow knew.

She didn't need to possess any kind of psychic ability to correctly read the suppressed excitement in his features.

So this was it. They would be leaving soon. His mind was probably already spinning as he made plans. For all she knew, he may even have made arrangements for a flight out tonight.

She sat beside him battling down a deep ache as he drove down the long driveway of The Sea Urchin, then turned in the direction toward Brambleberry House.

She wasn't ready for another loss so soon. She was still reeling from Abigail's death and now she would lose Eben and Chloe as well. How could she ever be happy in her quiet life without them?

She should never have let them so far into her world. It had been a huge mistake and she was very much afraid she would be paying the price for that particular error in judgment for a long time.

He would probably return to Cannon Beach at some point. She could at least console herself with that. His company had dozens of other hotels around the world, but The Sea Urchin was important to him, he had made no secret of it.

Now that she knew how much he cared about the hotel, she couldn't imagine him just buying the place for acquisition's sake alone. While Sage doubted he would have direct involvement in the future management of the hotel, she expected he would at least have some participation in decision-making.

Even if he left tonight, she knew it was unlikely she would never see him again.

In many ways, she almost thought she would prefer that alternative—that he leave Cannon Beach now that the papers were signed and never look back. How much harder would those occasional visits be, knowing she would have to steel herself to say goodbye to him again?

The rain had eased to a light, filmy drizzle. They were almost to Brambleberry House when she knew she had to say something.

"It's done, then?" she asked.

His brilliant, boyish smile cut through the darkness inside the Jaguar and, absurdly, made her want to weep. "It's done. The papers are signed. We'll need to have our attorneys go over everything in the morning but as far as I'm concerned, it's official."

"Congratulations."

She thought she had done a fairly credible job of cloaking her ambivalence behind enthusiasm, but some of it must have filtered through.

Eben sent her a swift look across the vehicle. "I know The Sea Urchin is a local landmark and has great meaning for the people of Cannon Beach. I've told you this before, but I think it bears repeating. I promise, I don't plan any major changes. A few coats of paint, maybe, a few modernizations here and there, but that's it."

"I believe you." She smiled, a little less feigned this time. "I'm thrilled for you, Eben. Really, I am. You got exactly what you wanted."

He opened his mouth to say something, then closed it again and she couldn't read his expression in the dim light. "Yes. Exactly what I wanted," he murmured.

"You said you had papers to sign tomorrow. I guess that means you're not leaving tonight, then?"

She saw his gaze shift to the rearview mirror, where Chloe was admiring her substantial pile of fortune cookies and not paying them any attention.

"No. We'll wait until the morning. The Wus and I will have to go through everything with the attorneys at The Sea Urchin first thing and then I'll have my pilot meet Chloe and me at the airport in Seaside when we're done."

She thought of the field trip they had planned all week for their last day of camp, to visit the Cape Meares Lighthouse and Wildlife Refuge. Chloe would be so disappointed to miss it but she knew Eben no doubt had many things to do back in the Bay Area and wouldn't delay for a little thing like a camp field trip.

As they reached Brambleberry House, some of Eben's excitement seemed to have dimmed—or perhaps he was merely containing it better.

Sage, on the other hand, felt ridiculously close to tears. She wasn't sure why, she only knew she couldn't bear the thought of saying goodbye to them in the car.

Besides that, Conan would never forgive her if she let them leave without giving him one last chance to see his beloved Chloe.

She injected an enthusiasm she was far from feeling into her voice. "Do you both want to come in for a few minutes? I've got a frozen cheesecake Abigail made me a...a few weeks before she died. I've been looking for a good occasion to enjoy it with some friends."

"I *love* cheesecake," Chloe offered from the backseat.

"You love anything with sugar in it, monkey."

She giggled at her father. "It's true. I do."

"It's settled, then." Sage smiled.

"Are you sure?" Eben asked.

"Absolutely. We need to celebrate. I'll have to take it out of the freezer but it should only take a few moments to thaw."

He seemed as reluctant as she for the evening to end. "Thank you, then," he said.

He reached behind the seat for the umbrella and came around to her door to open it for her. As he reached to help her from the vehicle, her nerves tingled at the touch of his hand.

"You and Chloe take the umbrella," he said. "You're the ones with the fancy dresses."

Sage found it particular bittersweet to hold Chloe's little hand tightly in hers as the two of them raced through the drizzle to the porch.

Oh, she would miss this darling child. Again she had to swallow down the ache in her throat.

Water droplets glistened in Eben's hair as he joined them on the porch while she unlocked the door.

"Is Conan upstairs or with Ms. Galvez?" Chloe asked when they were inside the entryway.

"He would have been lonely upstairs in my apartment by himself. I think he and Anna were watching a movie when I left."

"Can I take him upstairs with us for cheesecake?"

"Well, we can get him but I should warn you that Conan doesn't like cheesecake. His favorite dessert is definitely apple pie."

Chloe giggled, as Sage had intended. She kept her hand firmly in Sage's as they knocked on Anna's door.

For just an instant, Sage caught Eben watching her and she shivered at the glittery expression there.

Conan rushed through the door the moment Anna opened it. "Hey," Anna exclaimed. "How was dinner?"

"You know The Sea Urchin. It couldn't be anything other than exquisite," Sage answered. "Sorry to bother you but we're having an impromptu little party. I'm going to take out the frozen cheesecake Abigail made."

"What's the occasion?"

"We're celebrating," she said, forcing a smile. "Stanley and Jade agreed to sell to Spencer Hotels."

"Oh, that's wonderful! Congratulations."

Eben smiled, though in the better lighting of the entryway, Sage was certain he didn't look quite as thrilled as he had earlier.

"You and Conan have to join us while we celebrate," she said.

"May I look at the dolls first?" Chloe asked.

Anna sent a quick look at Sage and Eben. Her dark eyes danced with mischief for a moment in an expression that suddenly looked remarkably like one of Abigail's.

"Sure," she finally answered. "You two go ahead. Conan, Chloe and I will be up in a moment. Well, probably closer to ten or fifteen."

She ushered the girl into her apartment and closed the door firmly before Conan could bound up the stairs, leaving Eben and Sage alone in the entryway.

Feeling awkward—and more than a little mortified by Anna's not-so-subtle maneuvering to give her and

Eben some private time—Sage led the way up the stairs and into her apartment.

Eben closed the door behind him. She wasn't quite sure how he moved so quickly, but an instant later she was in his arms.

His kiss was firm, demanding, stealing the breath from her lungs. She wrapped her arms around him, exulting in his strength beneath her fingers, in the taste and scent of him.

For long, drugging moments, nothing else mattered but his mouth and his hands and the wild feelings inside her, fluttering to take flight.

"I've been dying to do that all night." His low voice sent shivers rippling down her spine.

She shivered and pulled his mouth back to hers, wondering if he could taste the edge of desperation in the kiss. She forgot about Chloe and Anna and Conan downstairs, she forgot about The Sea Urchin, she forgot everything but the wonder of being in his arms one more time.

One *last* time.

"I don't want to leave tomorrow."

At the ragged intensity of his voice, she blinked her eyes open. The reminder of her inevitable heartbreak seemed to jar her back into her senses.

What was the point in putting herself through this? The more she touched him, experienced the wild joy of being in his arms, the harder she knew it would be to wrench her heart away from him and return to her quiet, safe life before he and Chloe had stumbled into it.

She swallowed. "But you have to."

"I have to," he agreed, reluctance sliding through his voice. "I can't miss these Tokyo meetings."

He pressed his forehead to hers. "But I could try to rearrange my schedule to come back in a few weeks. A month on the outside."

She allowed herself a brief moment to imagine how it might be. Despite the heat they generated and these fragile emotions taking root in her heart, she knew she would merely be a convenience for him, never anything more than that.

She drew in a shuddering breath and slid out of his arms, desperate for space to regain her equilibrium. "I should, uh, get the cheesecake out of the freezer."

He raised an eyebrow at her deliberate evasion but said nothing, only followed her into the kitchen. She opened the small freezer and quickly found Abigail's foil-wrapped package.

Her hands shook a little as she pulled it out—from the embrace with Eben, but also from emotion. This was one more tie to Abigail that would be severed after tonight.

She looked at Abigail's handwriting on the foil with the date a few weeks before her death and one simple word: Celebrate.

Eben looked at the cheesecake from over her shoulder. He seemed to instinctively know how difficult it was for her to lose one more connection to Abigail. "Are you certain you don't want to save this a little longer, for some other occasion?"

She shook her head with determination. "I have the oddest feeling Abigail would approve. She was the one who introduced you to the Wus, after all. She never would have done that if she didn't want you to buy The Sea Urchin. I think she would be happy her cheesecake is being put to good use. In fact, if I know Abigail, she's probably somewhere lifting a glass of champagne to you right now."

He tilted his head and studied her for a long moment, then smiled softly. "I have you to thank as much as Abigail."

"I didn't do anything."

"Not true. You know it's not. I honestly think Stanley and Jade were ready to pull out until dinner tonight, until you and Chloe both charmed them."

He grabbed her fingers. "You reach Chloe in ways I don't think anyone has since her mother died."

She shifted and slid her hand away, uncomfortable with his praise. How could she tell him she understood Chloe's pain so intimately and connected with her only because her life had so closely mirrored the little girl's?

"What can I do to reach her that way?" Eben asked. By all appearances, he looked completely sincere. "You need to give me lessons."

"Just trust your instincts. That's the only lesson I can give."

"Following my instincts hasn't turned out well so far. Maybe if I had better success at this father business, I wouldn't have to send her to boarding school in the fall."

At first, she thought—hoped—she misheard him. He couldn't possibly be serious.

"Boarding school? You're sending her to *boarding school?*"

He shrugged, looking as if he wished he hadn't said anything. "Thinking about it. I haven't made a final decision."

"You have. Admit it."

She was suddenly trembling with fury. She was again eight years old, lost and alone, with no friends and a father who wanted little to do with her. "You've probably already signed her up and paid the first year's tuition, haven't you?"

Guilt flitted across his features. "A deposit, only to hold her spot. It's a very good school outside Newport, Rhode Island. My sister went there."

"Half a world away from you!"

"What do you want me to do, Sage? I've been at my wit's end. You've seen a different child this week than the one I've lived with for two years. Here, Chloe has been sweet and easygoing. Things are different at home. She's moody and angry and deceitful and nothing I do gets through to her. I told you she's been through half a dozen nannies and four different schools since her mother died. Every one of them says she has severe behavior problems and needs more structure and order. How am I supposed to give her that with my travel schedule?"

"You're the brilliant businessman. You don't need me to help you figure it out. Stop traveling so much or, if you have to go, take her with you. That's your answer, not dumping her off at some boarding school and then forgetting about her. She's a child, Eben. She needs her father."

"Don't you get it? I'm not the solution, I'm the damn problem."

As quickly as it swelled inside her, her anger trickled away at the despair in his voice. She longed, more than anything, to touch him again.

"Oh, Eben. You're not. She's a little girl who's lost her mother and she's desperate for her father's attention. Of course she's going to misbehave if that's the only time she can get a reaction from you. But she doesn't need a boarding school, she needs you."

"How do you know it won't help her?"

"Because I lived it! You want to know how I'm able to reach Chloe so well? Because I'm her with a few more years under my belt. I was exactly like Chloe, shunted away by my father to boarding school when I was eight simply because I no longer fit his lifestyle."

Chapter Thirteen

Eben stared at her. Of all the arguments he might have expected her to make, that particular one wouldn't have even made his list.

"Sage—"

She let out a long breath. Still in her party clothes, she looked fragile and heartbreakingly beautiful.

"My mother died when I was five," she went on. "I was seven when my father married his second wife, a lovely, extremely wealthy socialite who didn't appreciate being reminded of his previous wife and the life they had together. I was an inconvenience to both of them."

An inconvenience? How could anyone consider a child an inconvenience? For all his frustration with Chloe, none of it hinged on a word as cold as that one.

"I was dumped into boarding school when I was eight. The same age as Chloe. For the next decade, I saw my father about three weeks out of every year—one week during the Christmas holidays and two weeks in the summer."

He remembered her disdain for him early in their acquaintance, the contempt he saw in her eyes that first morning on the beach, the old pain he had seen in her eyes when they argued about whether he should take Chloe with him on his trip to Tokyo.

No wonder.

She thought of him as someone like her father, someone too busy for his own child. He ached to touch her but couldn't ignore the *hands-off* signals she was broadcasting around herself like a radio frequency.

"I'm so sorry, Sage."

Her chin lifted. "I survived. Listen to me complain like it was the worst thing that could ever happen to a child. It wasn't. I was always fed, clean, warm. I know many children endure much worse than an exclusive private boarding school in Europe. But I have to tell you, part of me has never recovered from that early sense of abandonment."

He pictured a younger version of Sage, lost and lonely, desperate for attention. He ached to imagine it.

But she was right, wasn't she? If he sent Chloe to boarding school, she would probably suffer some of those same emotions—perhaps for the rest of her life.

What the hell was he supposed to do?

"Boarding school doesn't have to be as you experienced it," he said. "My sister and I both went away for school when we were about Chloe's age. We did very well."

For him and, he suspected, for his sister, school had offered security and peace from the tumult and chaos of their home life. He had relished the structure and order he found there, the safety net of rules. He had thrived there in a way he never could have at home with his parents. In his heart, he supposed he was hoping Chloe would do the same.

"You don't have any scars at all?"

"A few." The inevitable hazings and peer cruelty had certainly left their mark until he'd found his feet. "But I don't know anyone who survives childhood without a scar or two."

"She's already lost her mother, Eben. No matter how lofty you tell yourselves your motives might be, I can promise that if you send Chloe away, she'll feel as if she's losing you, too."

"She won't be losing me. I'm not your father, Sage. I don't plan to send her away and ignore her for months at a time."

All his excitement at closing The Sea Urchin deal was gone now, washed away under this overwhelming tide of guilt and uncertainty.

"Besides, I told you I haven't made a final decision yet. This week has been different. *Chloe* has been different and I probably have been, too. If I can recapture that when we're back in our regular lives, there's no reason I have to follow through and send her to boarding school."

A small gasp sounded from the doorway. In the heat of the discussion with Sage—wrapped up in his dismay over inadvertently putting those shadows in her eyes—he had missed the sound of the door opening. Now, with a sinking heart, he turned to find Chloe standing there, her little features pale and her eyes huge and wounded.

"Chloe—"

"You're sending me to *boarding school?*" she practically shrieked. "You can't, Daddy. You *can't!*"

She was hitching her breath in and out rapidly, on the brink of what he feared would be a full-blown tantrum.

Helpless and frustrated, he went to her and tried to hug her, tangentially aware as he did so of Anna Galvez and Conan standing behind her in the hallway outside Sage's apartment.

"I didn't say I was sending you to boarding school."

She was prickly and resistant and immediately slid away from him. "You said you might not have to but that means you're thinking about it, doesn't it?"

He couldn't lie to her. Not about something as important as her future. "We don't have to talk about this right now. We're all tired and overexcited. Come on, let's have some of Sage's cheesecake."

"I don't want cheesecake! I don't want *anything*."

"Chloe—"

"I won't go! Do you hear me? I'll run away. I'll come here and live with Sage."

She burst into hard, heaving sobs and buried her face in Conan's fur. The dog licked her cheek then turned and glared at Eben.

Join the club, he thought. Everybody else in the room was furious with him.

He didn't know what to do, certain that if he tried to comfort his daughter he would only make this worse. To his vast relief, Sage stepped in and sat on the floor right there in the doorway in her elegant dress and pulled Chloe onto her lap.

She murmured soft, soothing words and after a few tense moments, Chloe's tears began to ease.

"I don't want to go to boarding school," she mumbled again.

"I know, baby."

Sage ran a hand over her hair but he noted she didn't give Chloe any false reassurances. "Do you think you're going to be up for cheesecake tonight? If you're not, you could always take some home with you."

"I'm not hungry now," Chloe whispered. "If it's okay with you, I'll take it home. Thank you."

By the time Sage cut into her friend's ironically labeled cheesecake—he had never felt *less* like celebrating—and packaged up two slices for them, Chloe had reverted to an icy, controlled calm that seemed oddly familiar. It took him a moment to realize she was emulating the way he tried to stuff down his emotions and keep control in tense situations.

Somebody ought to just stick a knife through his

heart, Eben thought. It would be far less painful in the long run than this whole parenting thing.

Anna had disappeared back to her apartment earlier during the worst of Chloe's outburst and Sage and Conan walked them down the stairs and to his car.

The rain had stopped, he saw. The night was cool and sweet with the scent of Abigail's flowers.

Chloe gave Sage an extra-long hug. If he wasn't mistaken, he saw Sage wipe her eyes after Chloe slid into the back seat, but when she lifted her gaze to his, it was filled with a Zen-like calm.

"This isn't the way I wanted the evening to end," he murmured. *Or the week, really.*

Their time with her had been magical and he hated to see it end.

He gazed at her features in the moonlight, lovely and exotic, and his chest ached again at the idea of leaving her.

"Will you come running with Chloe and me in the morning? Just one more time?"

She drew in a sharp breath. "I don't know if that's a good idea. It's late and Chloe probably will need sleep after tonight. Perhaps we should just say our goodbyes here."

"Please, Sage."

She closed her eyes. When she opened them, they brimmed with tears again and his heart shattered into a million pieces.

"I can't," she whispered. "Goodbye, Eben. Be well."

She turned and hurried up the sidewalk and slipped inside the house before he could even react.

After a long moment of staring after her, he climbed into the car, fighting the urge to press a hand to his chest to squeeze away the tight ache there.

Despite his halfhearted efforts to engage her in conversation, Chloe maintained an icy silence to him through the short distance to their rented beach house.

He couldn't blame her, he supposed. It had been a fairly brutal way to find out that he was considering sending her to boarding school. He had planned to broach the idea when he returned from Tokyo and slowly build to it over the summer, give her time to become adjusted to it.

"You know you're going to have to talk to me again sometime," he finally said when they walked to the door of their rented beach house. In answer, she pointedly turned her back, crossed her arms across her chest and clamped her lips shut.

He sighed as he unlocked the door and disengaged the security system. The moment they were inside, Chloe raced to her bedroom and slammed the door.

Eben stood for a moment in the foyer, his emotions a thick, heavy burden. He didn't know what the hell to do with them.

He needed a drink, he decided, and crossed to the small, well-stocked bar. A few moments later, snifter in hand, he sat in the small office calling his assistant to set up the meeting with his attorneys at The Sea Urchin in the morning and to arrange for the company Learjet to meet them at the airport in Seaside.

After he hung up, he sat for a moment wondering how a night that had started out holding such promise could have so quickly turned into an ugly disaster.

Now Sage was angry and disappointed in him, his daughter wasn't speaking to him, he was even getting the cold shoulder from a blasted dog, for heaven's sake.

The way his evening was going, he would probably be getting a phone call from the Wus telling him they had changed their minds *again*.

By the time he finished the tiny splash of brandy, he knew he had to face Chloe, if only to address her fears.

He knocked on her bedroom door. "Chloe? Let's talk about this. Come on."

Only silence met his knock. Surely she couldn't have fallen asleep already, could she? He knocked harder and tried the door, only to find it locked.

He didn't need this tonight. Frustration whipped through him and he banged even harder. "Chloe, open this door, young lady. Right now."

Still no answer. For the first time, unease began to filter through his frustration. He should never have let her come here and stew. It had been only a cowardly attempt to delay the inevitable. He should have just confronted the problem head-on the minute they walked into the house.

The lock on the bedroom door was flimsy. He quickly grabbed a butter knife from the kitchen, twisted the mechanism, then swung the door open.

A quick sweep of the darkened room showed the bed was still made, with no sign of his daughter.

"Chloe? Where are you hiding? This isn't funny."

He flipped on the light. The dress she had adored so much was discarded in a pile of taffeta on the floor and the shelves of the bureau were open, their contents spilling out, as if she had rummaged through looking for something in a hurry.

He barely saw any of that. His attention was suddenly focused on the curtains fluttering in the breeze and instantly Eben's unease turned to cold-edged fear.

The window was open to the sea-soaked night air and there was no sign of his daughter.

"Yeah, I know. I don't need a second piece of cheesecake. Or the first one, for that matter. You're one to talk. You pig out on *dog food*, for crying out loud."

Conan snickered and dipped his head back to his forepaws as he watched her lame attempts to drown her misery in a decadent swirl of sugar and cream cheese.

"It's not working, anyway," she muttered, setting the plate down on the coffee table in front of her.

She should be in bed, she knew. The day had been long, the evening painfully full and her muscles ached with exhaustion, but she knew she wouldn't be able to sleep.

Her emotions were too raw, too heavy. She had a sinking suspicion that when the sun rose, she would probably still be sitting right here on her couch in her bathrobe, red-eyed and wrung-out and three pounds heavier from the cheesecake.

Damn Eben Spencer anyway.

He had no business sweeping into her life, shaking up her status quo so dramatically, then riding off into the blasted sunset—especially not when her grief for Abigail still had such a stranglehold around her life.

Conan made a sad sound suddenly, as if he sensed she was thinking about his human companion.

He had seemed much less depressed these last few days with Eben and Chloe. How would their leaving affect him, poor dog? She had a feeling her quad muscles were in for some good workouts the next few mornings.

He had been acting strangely ever since Eben and Chloe had left for the evening. Now he stood again. Instead of going to the door to signal he needed to go out, he went to the windows overlooking the ocean and stared out into the night for a long moment then whined plaintively.

That was the third time he had repeated the same odd behavior in the last half-hour. It was starting to freak her out.

"What's the matter, bud?" she asked him.

Before the words were even out of her mouth, she heard a sharp knocking at the door downstairs.

Who on earth would be coming to call at—she checked her clock—eleven o'clock at night?

She went to the opposite windows but couldn't see a car in the driveway. The caller knocked again and Sage moved warily down the stairs, one hand on Conan's collar.

The best Conan would do was probably sniff an intruder to death but he was big and could look menacing if the light wasn't great and the intruder had bad eyes.

She left the chain in the door and peered through, but her self-protective instincts flew out into the night when she saw Eben standing on the porch, a frantic expression in his eyes.

"Eben! What is it? What's happened?"

He studied her for a moment, then raked a hand through his hair. "She's not here, is she?"

She blinked, trying to make sense of his appearance on her doorstep so late. "Chloe? No. I haven't seen her since the two of you left. She's not at home?"

"I thought she was just sulking in her bedroom. I gave her maybe twenty minutes to get it out of her system while I made a few calls. But when I went into her room to talk to her, she was gone and her window was open. I was certain she must have come here to find you. That's what she said, right? That she would run away and find you."

Conan whined and ran past them sniffing around the perimeter of the wrought-iron fence.

"You checked the beach?" Sage asked.

"That's the way I came. I ran the whole way, sure I would bump into her any minute, but I couldn't see any sign of her. I called and called but she didn't answer."

His eyes looked haunted. "I have to find her. Anything could happen to her alone in the middle of the night!"

His desperation terrified her as nothing else could. "Let me throw on some clothes and get a jacket and shoes. Perhaps we can split up, cover more ground."

Anna's door suddenly opened and she poked her

head out, her hair as messy as Sage had ever seen it and her dark eyes bleary with sleep. "What's wrong?"

"Sorry we woke you," Sage spoke quickly. "Chloe's missing. She was angry with her father about what happened earlier and it looks as if she snuck out her window."

She couldn't help but be impressed at the rapid way Anna pushed aside the cobwebs and became her normal brisk, businesslike self. "What can I do? Do you want me to call the police?"

Eben drew in a sharp breath. "I don't know. I just keep thinking she didn't have enough time to go far. Where could she have gone? There aren't that many places she's familiar with around here."

"I don't know. We've explored the area around here quite a bit this week in camp." Her voice trailed off and she gazed at Eben and saw the exact same realization hit him.

"Hug Point," Sage said. The beach they had visited when they took the tandem bicycle.

"Would she have time to get there?"

"She's fast. She could make it."

"That's a hell of a long way for an eight-year-old in the dark," Eben said, and she ached at the fledgling hope in his eyes.

"She has a flashlight. It's part of the survival kit we did the first day of camp."

"That must have been what she was rummaging through her room to find. That's something, isn't it?"

"Maybe." She paused, loathe to tell him more bad news but she knew she had no choice. "Eben, the tide is coming in fast. High tide will be in about ninety minutes."

She saw stark fear in his eyes and knew it mirrored her own.

"We should split up," he said. "One of us search down the beach in case she hasn't made it that far yet and is still on her way and the other one start at Hug Point and head back this direction."

"Good idea. I'll drive to Hug Point and start back-tracking this way. You take Conan with you."

She thought of the way the dog had immediately gone to Chloe that first day, as if he'd been looking just for her. "If she's out there, he'll help us find her."

"Okay."

She grabbed his hand, heartsore for him. "Eben, we'll find her."

He looked slightly buoyed by her faith and squeezed her fingers, then took off through the backyard to the beach access gate.

"Maybe I ought to call the police chief and give him a heads-up, just in case your hunch is wrong," Anna said.

"Do it," Sage said on her way up the stairs two at a time.

For all her reassurances to Eben, she knew exactly what dangers awaited a little girl on the beach in the dark at high tide and she couldn't bear to think of any of them.

Though it only took a few moments to reach Hug Point by car, it felt like a lifetime. The whole way, Sage gripped the steering wheel of her aging Toyota and tried to battle back her terror and her guilt.

She was as much to blame for this as Eben. If she hadn't overreacted so strongly at his mention of boarding school for Chloe, they wouldn't have been arguing about it and Chloe wouldn't have overheard.

It was none of her business what school Eben sent his daughter to. She had been presumptuous to think otherwise. In her usual misguided attempt to save the world, she had ended up hurting the situation far more than she helped.

She pulled into the parking lot as a light drizzle started again. Heedless of the rain or the wind that whipped the hood of her Gore-Tex jacket, she cupped her hands and called Chloe's name.

She strained hard to hear anything over the wind and the murmur of the sea. In the distance, somewhere beyond the headland, she thought she heard a small cry.

Though she knew well how deceiving sounds could be out here—for all she knew, it could have been a nocturnal shorebird—she decided she had to head in the direction of the sound.

In the dark, the shore was far different than it was in the daylight, though it had a harsh beauty here as well, like some wild moonscape, twisted and shaped by the elements.

She rounded the cluster of rocks, straining to see anything in the darkness.

She heard the same cry again and aimed her flashlight along the beach but it was a pitiful weapon to fight back the vast, unrelenting dark.

Suddenly on the wind, she could swear she heard Chloe's voice. "Help. Please!"

She turned the flashlight toward the water and her heart stopped when she saw several yards away a small figure in a pink jacket on one of the rocks they had played on the other day. She was surrounded by water now and the tide was rising quickly.

Far down the beach from the direction of Bramble-berry House, she saw a tiny spark of light on the beach and knew it was Eben. There wasn't time to wait for him but she whistled hard, hoping Conan would hear and come running. Perhaps Eben would pick up on the dog's urgency.

"I'm coming, baby," she called as she hurried down the sand. "Stay there. Just hang on."

When she was parallel on the shore with Chloe on her watery perch, she headed through the surf. She was prepared for the cold but it still clutched at her with icy fingers and she couldn't contain a gasp. No matter how cold she knew the ocean could be along the Pacific Northwest coast, even in June, it still took her by surprise.

She knew hypothermia could hit out here in a matter of minutes.

Chloe's rock was probably only twenty yards from shore but that seemed far enough as she waded through the icy water, now up to her knees. She was laboring for breath by the time she reached her. "Hi, sweetie,"

The sobbing girl threw her arms around Sage. She was wet and shivering and Sage knew she had to get her out of the water immediately.

"You came for me!" she sobbed. "I was so scared. I want my daddy."

Sage held her close and buried her face in the girl's hair, her heart full. She could barely breathe around the emotions racing through her.

"I know you want your daddy, honey. I know. He and Conan are coming down the beach from my house looking for you, but they'll be here in a minute. He'll be so happy to see you."

"Am I in big trouble?"

"What do you think?" she asked, trying to sound stern through her vast relief.

"I snuck out again, even though I promised I wouldn't. I went on the beach at night, even though you told me I shouldn't. I broke a lot of rules. I bet my dad's really mad."

Sage kept one eye on the rising tide. A wave hit her, soaking her to her waist and she knew they had to move. "Let's worry about that when we get out of here, okay? How about a piggyback ride?"

"Okay. My hands are really cold, though. I don't know if I can hang on."

"You can. Just pretend you're a crab and I'm your dinner and you don't want to let me go."

Chloe giggled and gripped her arms around Sage's neck. Sage could feel her shiver even through her jacket.

It was tough going on the way back. She couldn't see where she was going and she felt as if she were walking through quicksand. For the first time, she was grateful for the last month of morning runs that had built up her muscles. If not for those runs, she wasn't sure she would have had the endurance to get to shore.

A journey that had only been twenty yards on the way out now seemed like miles. They were almost to the sand when a sneaker wave came out of nowhere and slammed into the backs of her legs.

Tired and off balance with Chloe on her back, Sage swayed from the force of it and stumbled to her knees. She managed to keep her hold on Chloe but then another one washed over them and drove her face into the surf.

Spluttering and coughing, she wrenched her face free of the icy water. She had to get to her feet now, she knew, but she felt as if she were fighting the whole ocean.

At last, with a great surge of adrenaline, she staggered to her feet. Chloe was crying in earnest now.

"We're okay. We're okay. Only a little farther," she managed, then she heard the most welcome sounds she had ever heard—a dearly familiar bark and Eben's strong voice.

"Chloe! Sage!" he called. "Hang on. I'm coming."

She sobbed out a breath of relief and made it only another few feet before he reached them and guided them all back to safety.

Chapter Fourteen

By the time he reached them, both Sage and Chloe were soaked and shivering violently. He grabbed Chloe in one arm while he drew Sage against his body with the other. Together, the three of them made their way to the shore. Only when they were above the high tide line did Eben pause to take a breath.

His heart still pounded with rapid force from that terrible moment when he saw them both go down in the water and struggle so hard against the waves to come up.

"Are you both okay?" he asked.

In his arms, Chloe nodded and sniffled. "I'm sorry, Daddy. I'm sorry. I'm sorry. I shouldn't have run away. No wonder you want to send me away to boarding school."

He closed his eyes, pained that they had come back

to this. "We need to get you both warmed up. Come on. Let's get you home."

"There's a trail back to the road from here. That's probably the easiest way to get to the parking lot and my car."

After the longest fifteen minutes of his life, they made it to Sage's car.

"There's a b-blanket in the b-back for Chloe," she mumbled. "It's probably covered in dog hair but it's the b-best I can do."

He found it quickly and also a fleece jacket of Sage's, which he handed to her.

"I'll drive," he insisted. "You work on getting warm."

After Chloe was settled in the back wrapped in the blanket and cuddled next to Conan's heat, Eben climbed into the driver's seat and turned her heater on high.

His emotions were thick, jumbled, and his heart still pounded with remembered fear as he drove toward Brambleberry House.

"I should call Anna, tell her to call off the police," Sage said after a moment. Her trembling had mostly stopped, he saw with vast relief.

"The police were looking for me?" Chloe asked in a small voice from the back seat. "I'm in big trouble, aren't I?"

"Everybody was worried about you," Eben said.

Sage called Anna on her cell phone and for the next few moments their one-sided conversation was the only sound in the small vehicle.

"She's fine. We're all fine. Cold and wet but everybody's okay. Yeah, I'll be home in a minute. I'll tell her. Thanks, Anna."

She closed her phone and turned to the back seat. "Anna says to tell you she's so glad you're okay."

"Me, too," Chloe said sleepily. "I was so scared. The water wasn't high when I went out to the rock but then it started coming in fast and I didn't know what to do."

"You did the right thing to stay where you were," Sage said.

"I remembered what we talked about in camp. I tried to do just what you said."

He couldn't bear to think about what might have happened if Chloe hadn't had a little survival training through Sage's camp or if they hadn't found her in time.

With the resilience of the young, Chloe was nearly asleep by the time they reached Brambleberry House, her arms wrapped around Conan and her cheek resting against the top of his furry head.

He feared it would be as tough to wean her from the dog as it would be to leave this place.

"Just drop me off," Sage said. "I can pick up my car at your place tomorrow on my way to the center."

In the driveway, he put the car in park and finally reached for her hand. "Sage, I don't know how I can ever thank you."

She shook her head. "Don't. You know you don't need to thank me. I'm just so grateful everything turned out okay."

He was quiet for a moment, hot emotion choking his throat. He wanted to shunt it all away as he usually did, to lock it down deep inside him, but this wild tangle was too huge, to overwhelming.

He knew he couldn't leave things between them like this, tainted by this stilted awkwardness, not after everything that had happened.

"I know it's late but…I need to talk to you. After I get Chloe settled into bed, I would like to call Stanley and Jade, see if they could send someone over to stay with her for a little while."

She drew in a breath that ended in a little shiver, though he wasn't sure if it resulted from the cold or something else. "We don't really have anything left to say, do we?"

He squeezed her fingers. "I think we do. Please, Sage."

After an agonizingly long moment, she shrugged. "I'll try to watch for you so you don't have to ring the doorbell and wake Anna again."

He nodded. He had no idea what he wanted to say to her, he only knew he couldn't return home in the morning without seeing her again.

She opened the rear door for Conan and gave Chloe another hug, then hurried into her house.

Chloe said little as they drove back to their cottage. She was nearly asleep by the time he pulled into the driveway behind his rental, her head lolling back against the upholstery.

"Just a few more minutes, baby," he said as he helped

her inside. "A hot shower will help warm you up the rest of the way and wash away the saltwater."

She sighed. "I'd rather just go to bed. I'm so tired."

"I know, but you'll feel better, I promise. You're not going to fall asleep in there, are you?"

"No," she said, her voice subdued. "I'll be okay."

While he listened to the sounds of the shower, he changed out of wet khakis and shoes. He'd had it easy compared to Chloe and Sage and had only gotten wet up to mid-calf, but just that slight dousing left him cold.

He called The Sea Urchin front desk and, to his surprise, Jade answered. He left out a few details but explained he needed someone to come and sit with Chloe. Despite his best efforts to dissuade her, she insisted on coming herself and said she would be there in a few moments.

He was waiting in the living room when Chloe came out of the shower in her warmest flannel nightgown.

She hurried to him at once and wrapped her arms around his waist. She smelled sweet, like lavender soap and baby shampoo, and he held on tightly as more emotions caught in his throat.

"I really am super sorry I ran away, Daddy. I was just so mad at you but I wasn't thinking right."

He kissed the top of her head. "Trying to escape our problems doesn't work and usually only creates more trouble. Either they come right along with us or they're waiting where we left them when we get back."

She nodded, her damp hair leaving a mark against his shirt.

"I love you, baby," he said after a moment. "Please don't forget that. No matter what, I love you."

"I want to stay with you, Daddy. Please don't send me away. I'll try harder, I promise."

Sage had been right. He couldn't do it. Imperfect though he was—inadequate as he felt as a father—his daughter needed him.

"Same here, okay? I'll try harder, too. We both have to figure out how to make this work. I'll try to cut down my travel schedule so I'm home to spend more time with you."

"Oh, would you?"

More guilt sliced him at the stunned disbelief in her voice. "Yes. But you have to promise me that you'll settle down and work harder in school and that you'll take it easy on the new nanny when we get one."

Though she was about to fall over with exhaustion, she still managed to get a crafty look in her eyes. "Can I help pick her?"

"Well, I can't promise I'll let you make the final decision but you can have input. Deal?"

"Deal." She beamed at him. "I know just what I want. Somebody like Sage. She's pretty and she smells good and she's super nice."

That just about summed it up, Eben thought. "We'll have to see what we can do. I think Sage is one of a kind."

"You like her, too, don't you, Daddy?"

"Sure, baby." He wasn't quite ready to examine his emotions too closely—nor did he want to explain them to his eight-year-old daughter. Instead, he scooped her into his arms, earning a sleepy giggle.

"Come on, let's get you into bed, okay? Jade Wu is coming over to stay with you so I can take Sage's car back to Brambleberry House after you're asleep."

"Okay. Give Sage and Conan a big kiss for me, okay?"

He grimaced. He wasn't sure either of those creatures in question were very happy with him right now. "I'll see what I can do," he murmured as he tucked her into her bed, then kissed her forehead and slipped from the room to wait for Jade.

What the hell was he doing here?

Twenty minutes later, Eben drove Sage's car into the driveway of Brambleberry House, turned off the engine and sat for a moment in the dark silence.

He should just leave her car here, tuck the keys under the doormat and walk back down the beach. The smartest thing to do would be to leave things as they were and continue with his plans to leave in the morning.

But just the thought of it made him ache inside. He sighed, still not certain what he wanted to say to her.

He was still trying to puzzle it out when the porch light flipped on. A moment later, she opened the door and stood in the doorway, a slim, graceful silhouette, and his heart bumped in his chest.

Her hair was damp and she had a blanket wrapped around her shoulders and one hand on the dog. He let out a long breath and slid from the car. The night air was cool and moist from the rains earlier, sweet with Abigail's flowers and the salty undertone of the ocean.

Neither of them spoke until he reached the porch.

"I wasn't sure you were coming." Her voice was low and strummed down his spine as if she'd caressed his skin.

"I probably shouldn't have."

"Why are you here, then? You're not a man who does things he shouldn't."

He gave a rough laugh. "Aren't I?" Unable to resist, he stepped forward and framed her face in his hands. She was so achingly beautiful and the air eddying around them was sweetly magical and he had no choice but to kiss her.

She was perfect in his arms and as her mouth moved softly under his, he felt something tight and hard around his heart shudder and give way.

This was why he came. He knew it with sudden certainty. Because somehow when he was here, with this woman in his arms, all the tumult inside him seemed to go still.

He found a peace with Sage Benedetto he had never even realized had been missing in his life.

She wanted to cherish every second of this.

Sage twisted her arms around his neck, trying to burn each memory into her mind. She couldn't quite believe she had the chance to touch him and to taste him again when only a few short hours ago she thought he would be leaving her world forever.

"You're shivering," he murmured.

She knew it was in reaction to the wild chaos of emotions storming through her, but she couldn't tell him that. "I'm fine. My hair's just a little damp. That's all."

"You shouldn't be out here in the cool night air."

She was silent for a moment, gazing at the masculine features that had become so dear to her. "You're probably right," she finally murmured. "Come inside."

She knew exactly what she was offering—just as she knew she was signing herself up for even more heartache.

But she loved him. The truth of it had hit her the moment she saw him coming walking up the path. She was in love with Eben Spencer, billionaire hotelier and the last man on the planet a wild, flyaway nature girl from Oregon would ever have a forever-chance with.

This was all she would have with him and she couldn't make herself turn away now.

She walked up to her apartment without looking back. Over the pounding of her heart, she heard his footsteps behind her but he didn't say anything as they climbed the two flights of stairs.

Once inside, she frowned. She could swear she had left several lights on when she walked downstairs to let him in, but now only a single lamp was burning.

She had been reading while she waited and watched for him, listening to a Nanci Griffith CD but she must have bumped her stereo on her way out the door because now soft jazz played.

The whole room looked as if she had set the scene

for romance, which she absolutely had *not*. Despite her conviction that she wanted this, wanted him, she felt her face flame and hit the overhead light switch.

Nothing happened. The bulb must have burned out, she thought, mortified all over again.

Eben came into the room alone and she looked behind him. "Where's Conan?"

"I think he went through his door into Anna's apartment."

"Ah."

They stood looking at each other for a long moment and Sage could swear she could hear the churn of her blood pulsing through her body. She didn't think she had ever wanted anything in her life as much as she wanted him right now.

She opened her mouth to ask if he would like a drink or something—not that she had much, just some wine left over from the other night—but before any words could escape, he stepped forward and kissed her again.

Who needed alcohol when Eben Spencer was around? It was the last thought she had for a long time as she lost herself in the wonder of his strength, his touch.

After several long, glorious moments, he lifted his mouth away and pressed his forehead to hers. "I don't want to lose you, Sage."

She raised an eyebrow. "You can't lose what you don't have. An astute businessman like you should already know that."

He laughed, a low, amused sound that rippled over

her nerve endings. "You're very good at putting me in my place, aren't you?"

She smiled, liking the place he was in very, very much.

"I mean it," he said. "I have to leave in the morning but I don't want this to be the end for us."

She didn't want to think about his leaving or about the emptiness he would leave behind. "Eben—"

He stepped away from her, raw emotion on his face. He was usually a master at concealing his thoughts. To see him in such an unveiled moment shocked her.

He gripped her hands in his and brought them to his chest, where she could feel the wild pulse of his heartbeat. Had she done that to him? She wondered with surprise.

"I was terrified tonight," he said, his voice low. "I've never known anything like that."

"You were worried for your daughter," she said. "That was completely normal."

"My fear wasn't only for Chloe." His gaze locked with hers and she couldn't look away from the stunning tenderness in the glittery green depths of his eyes. "My world stopped when I saw that wave hit. All I could think was that I couldn't bear the thought of anything happening to either of you."

Sharp joy exploded inside her and she couldn't breathe around it.

"I care about you, Sage. You've become desperately important to me and to my daughter this week."

Close on the heels of the joy was an even bigger terror. This couldn't be real. Hadn't she just spent a week convincing herself of all the reasons there could never be anything between them?

"You'll go back to California and forget all about me."

"I don't think so." He brought their clasped hands to his mouth, his gaze still locked with hers. "I'm in love with you, Sage."

She swallowed, feeling lightheaded with shock. "You're not," she exclaimed.

"I've been fighting it with everything I have. Falling in love is not what I planned in my life right now—or ever."

He let go of her hands and stepped away from her. "My marriage was a mess, Sage. It taught me that love is complicated and confusing and…messy. I didn't want that again. I've done everything I can to talk myself out of it this week, but I can't deny it anymore. I'm in love with you, Sage. I don't want to be, but there it is. I think I have been since you showed up on my doorstep with Chloe that first morning."

I don't want to be in love with you.

She heard his words as if from a long distance, but they still managed to pierce the haze of disbelief around her.

He didn't want to love her. He had done all he could to talk himself out of it, had been fighting it with everything he had. He didn't want to be in love, didn't want the complications or the mess.

Panic fluttered through her and she was suddenly desperate for space to breathe, to think.

She couldn't do this. She *couldn't*. She had spent her childhood trying desperately to gain the attention of a man who didn't want to love her, who had shut his emotions off abruptly when he married her stepmother, leaving Sage with nothing.

She couldn't put herself through this again.

It was a simple matter of self-preservation. She loved him. The surety of it washed over her like the most powerful of sneaker waves.

She loved him and she knew all about how messy and painful love could be. She was terrified that she would give everything to Eben and he would destroy her.

She drew in a shaky breath and pressed a hand to her stomach, to the fear that roiled and churned there. He was watching her out of those vivid green eyes and she knew she had to say something.

Something cold and hard.

Final.

She was weak, desperate, and very much feared she had no willpower at all when it came to Eben Spencer.

"You're not in love with me, Eben. You're attracted to me, just as I am to you, but it's not love. How could it be? We barely know each other. We're far too different. We…we want different things out of life. You want to conquer the world and I want to clean it up and leave it a better place."

"A little simplistic, don't you think?"

She grabbed the blanket that had fallen during the heat of their embrace and wrapped it around her shoulders again, hoping he wouldn't notice her trembling.

"Maybe it is simplistic. But look at us! You're the CEO

of a billion-dollar hotel dynasty and I'm perfectly happy here in my little world, showing kids how to tell the difference between a clingfish and a sculpin. When you think about it, you have to see we have nothing in common."

"We can get past the few differences between us."

"I don't *want* to get past them."

For once in her life, she desperately wished she were a better liar. She could only pray he wouldn't look closely enough to see right through her. "I'm physically attracted to you, Eben, I can't deny that. I'm attracted to you and I adore Chloe. But I'm…I'm not in love with you. You're not the kind of man I want."

She was trembling in earnest now, sick with the lie and had to pull the blanket tighter around her shoulders to hide it from him.

He gazed at her for a long moment and she forced herself to lift her chin and return his gaze, praying she could keep all trace of emotion from her features.

"Fair enough," he finally said, his voice quiet. "I guess that's all that really matters, isn't it?"

A few more moments, she told herself. *Keep it together just a few more moments and he'll be gone.*

"I'm sorry," she murmured.

His laugh was rough, humorless. "You don't have to apologize for not sharing my feelings, Sage. I told you love was messy. There's nothing messier than one person feeling things that aren't returned."

She could say nothing, could only clutch the blanket around her with nerveless fingers.

"I guess this is goodbye, then," he said, reaching for the doorknob. "I have to come back to Cannon Beach. There's no avoiding that—I just bought a hotel here. But on the rare occasions I come back to oversee the transition of The Sea Urchin to Spencer Hotels ownership, I'll do my best to stay out of your way."

She thought her heart would crack apart again. How many times was she going to have to say goodbye to him? She couldn't bear this. "You don't have to do that."

One corner of his mouth lifted in a grim ghost of a smile. "Yeah. Yeah, I do."

He opened the door but turned back before he passed through it for the last time. "Goodbye, Sage. Thank you again for tonight, for Chloe. You gave me back my daughter and I don't just mean by rescuing her from the tide. I'm not sending her to school, if that makes you feel any better. The two of us will tough it out and try to figure things out together."

"That's good. I'm happy for you both."

Oh, please go! She couldn't bear this.

He gave that ghost of a smile again then walked out, closing the door behind him.

She managed to keep it together, her hands gripping the blanket tightly while she listened to his footsteps down the stairs and then the creak of the outside door opening and closing.

She waited a few more moments, until she could be certain he was on his way back to his beach house, then a wild sob escaped her, then another and another.

By the time Conan climbed the stairs a few moments later, she had collapsed on the couch and was sobbing in earnest.

Her dog raced into the room, sniffed around the entire apartment, then barked. She opened her gritty eyes to find him giving her what she could only describe as an accusing stare.

She was *not* in the mood to deal with another contrary male.

"Don't look at me like that," she tried to snap, though it came out more like a wail. "You're supposed to be on my side, aren't you?"

Conan barked and she could swear he shook his head.

"It's better this way. You're smart enough to know that," she muttered. "It never would have worked out. We're just too different. Eventually he would figure out I'm not what he needs or wants. I can't go through that. You understand, don't you? I *can't*."

She knew the tears she was wiping away probably negated some of the resoluteness of her voice but she couldn't seem to make them stop.

After another moment of glaring at her, Conan made a snorting, disgusted kind of sound. She thought he would amble back down to Anna's apartment. Instead, he came to her and licked at the tears on her cheeks, then settled beside her.

Sage wrapped her arms around his solid mass and wept.

Chapter Fifteen

She finally fell into a fitful sleep sometime in the early hours of the morning, only to be awakened a short time later by a cold nose snuffling the side of her neck.

"Oh, for the love of Pete," she grunted. "Why don't you go harass Anna for once?"

Now the cold nose was joined by a paw on her shoulder. Conan threw in a whine for good measure.

She glanced at her alarm clock. Six o'clock. He'd at least given her an extra half-hour of sleep. She supposed she ought to be grateful for that much. She scrubbed at her face with one hand and sat up. Every single muscle in her body ached.

Her penance, she supposed, for a night of only a few

moments' sleep. Conan whined impatiently at the emerging signs of life from her.

She frowned at him. "I guess a broken heart doesn't win me any amnesty when it comes to your daily run, does it?"

He moved his head from side to side in that uncanny way he had. Obstinate male. He barked and cocked his head toward the door. *Come on. Let's go, lazybones.*

For a nonverbal creature, he was remarkably communicative. She sighed, surrendering to the inevitable. She had to be up soon for work anyway. Perhaps a few moments of fresh sea air would help clear this wool from her head.

Ten minutes later, still aching and exhausted but now in her workout clothes, her hair yanked back into a ponytail, she followed Conan down the stairs at a much slower pace than his eager gallop.

Outside, the sun was just beginning its rise above the Coast Range. The sweetness of Abigail's flowers mingled with the sharp, citrusy scent of the Sitka spruce and pines. It was a beautiful morning. She only wished she had room in her heart past this pain to enjoy it.

Still, the cool air did help her wake up and by the time she propped open the beach access gate and took off across the sand, she was moving a little less gingerly.

As usual, the moment they hit the beach, he tugged the leash for her to head downtown—exactly the direction she did not want to go. She couldn't take the chance that Eben might be outside his beach house again. She just couldn't face him this morning.

Or ever.

"No, bud. This way."

Conan barked and kept going to the very limit of his retractable leash. She managed to find the strength to give him the resistance to keep him from dragging her up the beach with him.

Sage pointed stubbornly in the other direction, as far away from Eben's beach house as she could get. "This way," she repeated.

Conan whined but had no choice but to comply. When she started a halfhearted jog down the beach, he came along with a huffy reluctance that might have made her smile under other circumstances.

"It's no fun when somebody makes you go somewhere you don't want to, is it?" she muttered, wondering if his keen communication skills stretched to understanding irony.

After a few moments of running, she had to admit she felt slightly better. The slanted light of day breaking across the wild, rugged shoreline didn't calm her soul, but at least the endorphins helped take the edge off the worst of her despair.

She had the grim feeling it would take many more of these morning runs before she could find the peace her heart needed.

Why did Eben and Chloe have to come into her life now—and leave it again—when she was still reeling from losing Abigail? It hardly seemed fair.

If she had met them both before Abigail died, would

she have even let them into her life? She didn't know. Perhaps she wouldn't have been as vulnerable to falling for both of them if her emotions hadn't been so raw and unprotected.

No, that was a cop-out. She had a feeling she would have fallen hard for them no matter what the circumstances. Chloe was completely irresistible and Eben... well, Eben reached her heart in ways no man ever had.

Or ever would again, she was very much afraid.

She sobbed out a little breath. Just from exertion, she told herself. It was good for her. Maybe if she ran hard enough, she could outpace the pain.

The tide rose and fell on Oregon's coast approximately every twelve hours. It was almost low tide now, the perfect time for beachcombing. She passed a few early-morning adventurers as she ran, most of them tourists who waved at her and smiled at Conan's friendly bark.

After a mile and a half, she stopped, her breath heaving in her lungs. That first rush of endorphins could only take her so far. She wasn't up for their full five-mile round trip, she decided. Three would have to do for today. She started to turn around, when suddenly Conan barked sharply and tugged his leash so hard he nearly toppled her into the sand.

"What's the matter with you?" She pulled after him to follow her but he gave another powerful lunge away from her and the leash slipped out of her perspiration-slicked hands.

In seconds, he was gone, tearing down the beach in the direction of Hug Point.

"Conan, get back here!" she yelled, but he completely ignored her, racing toward a couple of beachcombers several hundred yards away.

He was going to scare the life out of them if he raced up to them at full-speed, a big hairy red beast rocketing out of nowhere. She had to hope it wasn't a couple of senior citizens with an aversion to dogs and a team of attorneys on retainer.

She groaned and hurried after him.

"Conan! Get back here."

From here, she saw him jump all over one of them and she groaned.

And then she saw a small figure hugging Conan, heard a high, girlish giggle drift toward her on the breeze, and her heart seemed to stop. She shifted her gaze to see the other person on the beach who stood watching her approach, his dark hair gleaming in the dawn.

Eben and Chloe.

She wanted to turn and run hard in the other direction. She couldn't handle this. Not now. She needed time to restore the emotional reserves that had been depleted by her crying jag the night before.

Were her eyes as puffy and red as they felt? Oh, she hoped not.

It was far too late to turn and run back to the safety of Brambleberry House. Conan was already wriggling around them both with enthusiasm and Chloe was waving for all she was worth.

"Sage! Hi Sage!"

Somehow from deep inside her, she dug around until she found the courage to meet Eben's gaze. His features were impassive and revealed nothing as he watched her approach.

I'm in love with you.

For an instant, she could hear nothing but those words, not even the low murmur of the ocean.

He had offered her a priceless gift and she had rejected it with cruel finality.

I don't love you. You're not the kind of man I want.

She wanted to sob all over again at the lie. How could she face him in the cold light of day?

She looked away quickly and turned her attention back to Chloe. "Hey. Good morning. I didn't expect to see you today."

Or you can bet I would have been back at my house with the covers over my head right now.

"My dad woke me up. He said we had to try to find a few more sand dollars to take home today so we can always remember our trip together. Look at how many we have. He's the best at finding them."

"You're lucky to get them before the gulls do. That's terrific."

"I'm going to make something cool with them. I don't know what yet but I'll figure something out."

"Great."

Oh, she did not want to be here. She wanted to grab her dog and run as far and as fast as they could until both of them collapsed in the sand.

"Look! My dad doesn't have his shoes on, either. Don't you think that's funny? He said he wanted to wriggle his toes in the sand one more time before we leave."

Against her will, Sage shifted her attention to Eben and saw that, indeed, his bare feet were covered in sand. She couldn't seem to look away from the sight.

"This isn't going to last long." His voice sounded tight, slightly strangled, and her gaze flew to his. A glimmer of emotion slipped through his steely reserve and she could swear he looked as if this was as awkward for him as it was for her. "To be honest, it's not what I expected. The sand is much colder than I thought it would be and I'm a little nervous about being pinched by a hermit crab."

"But you tried it, just like you said you wanted to, didn't you, Daddy?" Chloe chirped, oblivious to the currents zinging between them.

He smiled, more than a little self-consciousness in his expression, his eyes shimmering with love for his daughter.

As she gazed at him, something inside her seemed to shatter apart.

The stiff, controlled businessman she had mistaken him for early in their relationship was nowhere in sight. She was stunned by the transformation. His jeans were rolled up, his toes were bare and he had his hands full of sand dollars.

She thought of him that first day when she had taken Chloe home to their beach house. He had been angry and humorless and she never would have imagined in a million years that one day she would find him digging his toes in the sand, laughing with his daughter, hunting for the treasures delivered the sea.

Or that she would come to love him so dearly.

"Did *you* get pinched by a crab?" Chloe asked her. "You look funny."

Everything inside her began a slow, achy tremble and she suddenly felt as if her heart was like one of the gulls overhead, wheeling and diving across the sky.

"I'm…I'm fine."

Her voice sounded scratchy, and drew Eben's gaze. She saw echoes of longing in his eyes and a pain that matched her own.

She let out a breath, trying so hard to hang on to some shred of sanity. Nothing had changed. Not really. She was still terrified she would be left bruised and bloody.

No. She gazed at his bare feet and at the sight of them, it seemed as if her fear ebbed out to sea with the tide.

She loved him. More than that, she trusted him. He might not be comfortable digging his feet into the sand, but he had done it for his daughter's sake. And for his own. Because he wanted to know what it was like, even if it wasn't the most comfortable feeling in the world.

He was a good man. A wonderful man. If she didn't reach for the priceless gift he had offered her, she suddenly knew she would spend every moment of the rest of her life regretting it.

She wanted desperately to tell him but knew she

could say nothing in front of Chloe. As if reading her mind, Conan, bless him, suddenly barked and took off after a gull down the beach.

"Hey! Get back here," Chloe giggled, running after him.

"I'm sorry," Eben finally said when the two of them were alone. He sat on a rock and started slipping his shoes back on. "I assumed with the late night and…everything…that you and Conan probably wouldn't be running this morning. I didn't mean to make you uncomfortable by forcing you to have to see us again."

She shook her head. "I'm not uncomfortable."

"No?" He rose from the rock. "Well, that makes one of us."

How difficult must it be for him to meet up with the woman who had coldly rejected him the night before?

"Don't be uncomfortable. Please."

"Sorry. I haven't had a lot of experience with this. I'm not exactly sure the correct protocol here. How does a man act smooth and urbane around the woman in front of whom he's made a complete ass of himself?"

She closed her eyes, hating the echo of hurt in his voice. She couldn't do this. She had to tell him the truth, no matter how painful.

"I lied, okay?" she finally blurted out. "I lied."

A dead silence met her pronouncement, with no sound at all but the waves and the gulls overhead.

"You…lied about what?"

She went to him and reached for his hand, wishing

she wasn't disheveled and sweaty for this. He seemed to always see her at her worst.

Yet he loved her anyway.

"I lied when I told you you weren't the kind of man I want, that I didn't love you. I've never told such a shocking untruth."

He suddenly looked as astonished as if she had just knocked him into the cold waves.

"You don't have to do this."

"Yes, I do." She squeezed his fingers. "I love you, Eben. I have from the beginning."

"Sage—"

She didn't give him time to say anything, just blurted out the rest. "I'm such a coward. I never realized that about myself until last night. I always thought I had everything figured out, that I was so in control of my world. I thought I had worked through all the stuff of my past and become a capable, well-adjusted adult."

"You are."

She shook her head, fighting tears. "No. Inside I'm eight years old again, watching my father walk away without a backward look. I was so afraid to admit my feelings, a-afraid to give you that same kind of power to hurt me. Instead, I decided I would be the one doing the walking."

He said nothing, just continued to watch her, as if he didn't quite know what to believe.

She drew in a breath and reached for his other hand.

"I love you, Eben. I'm sorry if I...hurt you by lying and saying I didn't."

He gazed at her for one stunned moment and then he gave a little, disbelieving laugh and tugged her into his arms. As his hard mouth covered hers, Sage wrapped her arms around his waist and held on for dear life. The tight ache inside her eased and she could finally breathe again, for the first time in hours.

This was right. This was exactly where she belonged, right here in his arms.

"It was ripping my heart out to leave you," he murmured against her mouth. "I came down to the beach with Chloe one more time because I wanted one last connection to you. I felt closer to you here by the ocean than anywhere."

She kissed him again and the tenderness in his touch brought tears to her eyes.

"Don't cry," Eben murmured, kissing her cheeks where a few tears trickled down.

She laughed, wondering if her heart could burst from happiness. "These are happy tears. Not like the ones I cried all night. Conan had to drag me out of bed to run. All I wanted to do was pull the covers over my head and hibernate there for a few weeks."

"What if I'd missed you this morning?" he asked. "If I hadn't decided to bring Chloe here one last time? If you and Conan had decided to go in the other direction?"

She hugged him. "We're both here. That's the important thing."

"I think you're the reason I came back for The Sea Urchin, why it seemed so vital to me that I buy it. The hotel was only part of it. Call it fate or destiny or dharma or whatever, but I think everything that's happened was leading me right here, to this moment and to you."

It was the perfect thing to say and she could swear she tumbled even deeper in love with him. This was her prosaic, austere businessman, talking of fate and destiny? Dharma? Had she ever been so wrong about a person in her life?

"I think it was Abigail."

He blinked. "Abigail?"

"I think she met you and fell for those gorgeous green eyes of yours."

She could swear a touch of color dusted his cheek-bones. "She did not."

"You didn't know her as well as I did. She always was a sucker for a gorgeous man. Since she couldn't have you for herself, I think she handpicked you for me and she's been doing everything she can since she met you to throw the two of us together."

Eben didn't look convinced, but since he reached for her and kissed her again, she decided the point wasn't worth arguing.

She received confirmation of it a moment later, though, when a sudden bark managed to pierce the lovely fog of desire swirling around her. She wrenched her mouth from Eben's to gaze at her dog.

Conan watched them from a few feet away with that uncanny intelligence in his eyes. He barked again, a delighted sound. It seemed ridiculous, but she could swear he looked pleased.

Chloe was close on the dog's heels and she studied them with startled concern in her green eyes. "Daddy, why are you holding on to Sage? Did she fall?"

His expression filled with sudden panic, as if he hadn't quite thought far enough ahead about explaining this to his daughter. Sage took pity on him and stepped in.

"You're exactly right. I fell, really hard. Harder than I ever thought I could. But you know what? Your dad was right there to pick me back up and help me find my feet. Isn't that lucky?"

Chloe's brow furrowed as she tried to sift through the layers of the explanation. Sage could tell she wasn't quite buying it. "So why is he still holding on to you?"

She laughed and slanted Eben a look out of the corner of her eyes. "I'll let you answer that one," she murmured.

He gave her a mock glare then turned to his daughter, "Well, after I helped her up, I discovered I didn't want to let her go."

Chloe seemed to accept that with surprising equanimity. She studied them for a moment longer, then shrugged. "You guys are weird," she finally said, then chased Conan across the sand again.

"I meant it. I *don't* want to let you go," Eben repeated fiercely after they were gone.

She wrapped her arms around his neck and held on tight. "I'm not going anywhere."

As he kissed her again, she could swear she heard Abigail's wicked laughter on the wind.

HARLEQUIN *Romance*.

New York Times bestselling author

DIANA PALMER

Handsome, eligible ranch owner Stuart York knew
Ivy Conley was too young for him, so he closed his heart
to her and sent her away—despite the fireworks between
them. Now, years later, Ivy is determined not to be
treated like a little girl anymore…but for some reason,
Stuart is always fighting her battles for her. And safe in
Stuart's arms makes Ivy feel like a woman…his woman.

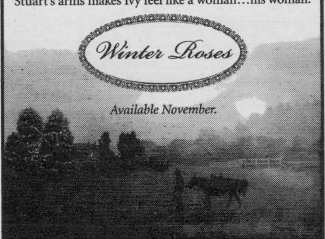

Winter Roses

Available November.

Cut from the soap opera that made her a star, America's TV goddess Gloria Hart heads back to her childhood home to regroup. But when a car crash maroons her in small-town Mississippi, it's local housewife Jenny Miller to the rescue. Soon these two very different women, together with Gloria's sassy assistant, become fast friends, realizing that they bring out a certain secret something in each other that men find irresistible!

Look for

THE SECRET GODDESS CODE

by

PEGGY WEBB

Available November wherever you buy books.

Romantic
SUSPENSE

Sparked by Danger, Fueled by Passion.

Onyxx agent Sully Paxton's only chance of
survival lies in the hands of his enemy's daughter
Melita Krizova. He doesn't know he's a pawn in the
beautiful island girl's own plan for escape. Can
they survive their ruses and their fiery attraction?

*Look for the next installment in the
Spy Games miniseries,*

Sleeping with Danger
by Wendy Rosnau

Available November 2007 wherever you buy books.

COMING NEXT MONTH

#1861 A FAMILY FOR THE HOLIDAYS—Victoria Pade
Montana Mavericks: Striking It Rich
Widow Shandie Solomon moved to Montana with her infant daughter
for a new lease on life—and got one, when she opened her beauty
parlor next door to Dex Traub's motorcycle shop. By Christmastime
the bad boy of Thunder Canyon had Shandie hooked…and she
couldn't tell if it was sleigh bells or wedding bells ringing in her future.

#1862 THE SHEIK AND THE CHRISTMAS BRIDE—
Susan Mallery
Desert Rogues
Prince As'ad of El Deharia agreed to adopt three orphaned American
girls on one condition—that their teacher Kayleen James take over
as nanny. In a heartbeat the young ladies turned the playboy prince's
household upside down…and Kayleen turned his head. Now he would
do anything to keep her—and make her his Christmas bride!

#1863 CAPTURING THE MILLIONAIRE—Marie Ferrarella
The Sons of Lily Moreau
It was a dark and stormy night…when lawyer Alain Dulac crashed his
BMW into a tree, and local veterinarian Kayla McKenna came to his
aid. Used to rescuing dogs and cats, Kayla didn't know what to make
of this strange new animal—but his magnetism was undeniable. Did
she have what it took to add this inveterate bachelor to her menagerie?

#1864 DEAR SANTA—Karen Templeton
Guys and Daughters
Investment guru Grant Braeburn had his hands full juggling stock
portfolios and his feisty four-year-old daughter, Haley. So the distant
widower reluctantly turned to his former wife's flighty best friend
Mia Vaccaro for help. Soon Haley's Christmas list included marriage
between her daddy and Mia. But would Santa deliver the goods?

#1865 THE PRINCESS AND THE COWBOY—Lois Faye Dyer
The Hunt for Cinderella
Before rancher Justin Hunt settled for a marriage of convenience that
would entitle him to inherit a fortune, he went to see the estranged
love of his life, Lily Spencer, one more time—and discovered he was
a father. Could the owner of Princess Lily's Lingerie and the superrich
cowboy overcome their volatile emotions and make love work this time?

#1866 DÉJÀ YOU—Lynda Sandoval
Return to Troublesome Gulch
When a fatal apartment blaze had firefighter Erin DeLuca seeing red
over memories of her prom-night car accident that took her fiancé
and unborn child years ago, ironically, it was pyrotechnics engineer
Nate Walker who comforted her. At least for one night. Now, if only
they could make the fireworks last longer…

SSECNM1007